Maybe now was the time to be honest with him.

"I've promised never to love someone that fights fires or works in a dangerous profession again. It's nothing personal, Jared. But I just can't go through the pain of losing someone again."

It was better this way. Better for Jared, too.

So, why did she suddenly feel so lost and forlorn?

He went very still. "And that includes me?"

She looked down and swallowed hard. She didn't answer. She didn't need to.

"Well, at least you're being honest with me," he said.

She looked up. "I'm sorry, Jared. I don't mean to hurt your feelings. It's just that I've got two kids to worry about. I've got to put their needs first."

His eyes crinkled in a smile of understanding, but she saw the pain in his eyes. "Believe me, I get it. But I'm not convinced I'm bad for you and those kids. I'm good for you, lady. You just can't see it, yet. And I'm going to try my hardest to convince you that you need me."

Leigh Bale is a *Publishers Weekly* bestselling author. She is the winner of the prestigious Golden Heart® Award and is a finalist for the Gayle Wilson Award of Excellence and the Booksellers' Best Award. The daughter of a retired US forest ranger, she holds a BA in history. Married in 1981 to the love of her life, Leigh and her professor husband have two children and two grandkids. You can reach her at leighbale.com.

Books by Leigh Bale

Love Inspired

Men of Wildfire

Her Firefighter Hero

Lone Star Cowboy League

A Doctor for the Nanny

The Healing Place
The Forever Family
The Road to Forgiveness
The Forest Ranger's Promise
The Forest Ranger's Husband
The Forest Ranger's Child
Falling for the Forest Ranger
Healing the Forest Ranger
The Forest Ranger's Return
The Forest Ranger's Christmas
The Forest Ranger's Rescue

Her Firefighter Hero

Leigh Bale

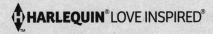

Recycling programs for this product may not exist in your area.

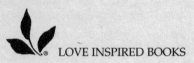

LOVE INSPIRED BOOKS

ISBN-13: 978-0-373-81909-6

Her Firefighter Hero

Copyright © 2016 by Lora Lee Bale

This is a work of fiction. Names, characters, places and incidents are either the product of the author's imagination or are used fictitiously, and any resemblance to actual persons, living or dead, business establishments, events or locales is entirely coincidental.

This edition published by arrangement with Love Inspired Books.

® and TM are trademarks of Love Inspired Books, used under license. Trademarks indicated with ® are registered in the United States Patent and Trademark Office, the Canadian Intellectual Property Office and in other countries.

www.Harlequin.com

Printed in U.S.A.

There is no fear in love;
but perfect love casteth out fear...
—*1 John* 4:18

This book is dedicated to my Jared,
who adores my daughter as we adore him.

Chapter One

"Order up!" Megan Rocklin slid a plate of scrambled eggs, bacon and hash browns beneath the warming lamp. As she wiped her damp hands on a clean dish towel, she took a quick glance at the tables in the diner. All but two were full, and the place buzzed with the happy chatter of satisfied customers. Not bad, considering she owned the only restaurant in town. If only it were this busy every other day of the week, she could pay off a few bills and breathe a bit easier.

Turning back to the grill, she picked up a spatula and flipped a series of pancakes. The air smelled of breakfast, warm and nice. It was her favorite part of the day. But she still needed to slice vegetables and fruit for the afternoon salad bar.

She slid open the glass pane of the window and welcomed the gush of fresh April air. Blazing sunshine taunted her. She'd like nothing more than to close up the diner, load her two kids and a picnic lunch into their rusty old truck and drive the twenty miles to Duck Creek Park. But taking a day off work was a luxury she couldn't afford right now. She'd graduated from one of the top culinary schools in the nation, and look where she'd ended up. Living in the small, remote town of Minoa, Nevada.

Speaking of which. Where was Frank? The cook's ten-minute break should have ended five minutes ago.

Megan tossed an irritated glance toward the back door. No doubt he was outside in the alleyway, puffing on a cigarette. She wouldn't complain, though. Frank worked long hours without protest. A good, solid employee. She was just tired and grouchy, that's all.

She forked a giant ham steak off the grill, slapped some eggs over easy and thick fries on the side, and garnished the plate with a slice of orange. Through the cutout window to the restaurant, she caught a glimpse of Connie racing back and forth to take orders, shuffle food and refill drinks. Megan should be out there helping her.

Blinking her gritty eyes, she gave the pancakes another flip. From all outward appearances, she didn't miss a beat. But inwardly, her arms and legs felt like leaden weights. She hadn't slept well the night before. In fact, she rarely slept through the night these days. Not since Blaine's death last summer. And boy! Did she ever miss him today.

"So, what have we got?" Frank lumbered into the kitchen, a burly man of forty-eight years. Pulling his chef's hat onto his balding head, he gave a deep, hacking cough. At least he covered his mouth. An invisible fog of cigarette smoke seemed to follow him as he stepped over to the double ovens. Megan hid a grimace.

"That bad habit of yours is gonna kill you one of these days, Frank. I wish you'd give it up," she said.

She meant well but tried not to sound too much like his mother. Lately, she sounded like everyone's mom. An old harpy, that's what she'd become. She figured if she held on tight enough, she could control the world around her and keep from being hurt again. Her common sense told her that was an insane notion, yet she couldn't let go completely and allow herself to be the happy, naive woman she'd once been. Not as a widow with two kids to raise and plenty of bills to pay.

"I know it's not good for me, but now that my Martha's gone, I ain't got nothing but this job to live for," Frank said.

His words sank deep into her heart. Blaine was gone, too, but at least she still had Caleb and June, her five-and eight-year-old children. If not for them, she wouldn't have much to live for, either. And life shouldn't be that way. Not ever.

"You've always got a place here with us, Frank. You mean a lot to me, which is why I wish you'd give up those cigarettes." She reached up and squeezed his arm affectionately, meaning every word.

"Thanks, ma'am." He flashed an unassuming grin, his ruddy cheeks wobbling.

She handed him the pancake turner. "You've got biscuits in the oven ready to come out and cakes on the grill ready to come off right now. And we're out of sourdough."

He didn't bat an eye but went right to work assembling plates of food like a pro. Always calm, always steady. Megan thought she could learn something from his example. Outwardly, she appeared serene and collected. But inside, she was screaming. Too much work. Too little money. Too little sleep. And way too lonely.

The truth was, she didn't want to be a sin-

gle mom. She shouldn't be a young widow.
There was so much life ahead of her. So much
love she wanted to share. But one thing was
certain. She'd never, ever love another man
that worked in a dangerous profession. After
losing her husband fighting wildfires last
summer, her heart couldn't take it. No, sirree. Not ever again.

Stepping out into the restaurant, Megan
reached behind the front counter for the coffeepot and made the rounds at each table, refilling cup after cup.

"Thanks, babe," Connie trilled as she
zipped past carrying four steaming plates of
food.

Besides waitressing, Connie was also her
dear friend. And after Blaine's death, she'd
been there for Megan. A sympathetic shoulder to cry on. Comforting and encouraging.
Someone Megan could confide in.

"No problem," Megan called in a light
voice. "Just think. Only nine more hours and
we can all go home."

"You've got nine hours, but I've got just
five," Connie shot back with a laugh.

Yeah, Megan was abundantly aware of that
fact. She'd opened the restaurant at six that
morning and would be here until it closed at
nine that evening.

She pushed that weary thought aside and reminded herself that she had a lot to be grateful for. It hadn't been easy, but God had taken care of them.

The bell over the door tinkled, heralding the arrival of another customer. A tall, well-built man stepped inside. In a room filled with people, Megan felt his presence even before she glanced up. Her mouth dropped open and she stared. Not because he was a stranger, but because of how he looked.

High cheekbones, a chiseled chin, dark blond hair and devil-may-care eyes. More handsome than a man had a right to be. The kind that could have walked straight off the cover of *GQ* magazine. His blue jeans, cowboy boots and white T-shirt hugged his muscular body to perfection. Tall, lean and strong, he glanced about the room, taking it all in with a confident lift of his head. He radiated self-assurance. As though he owned the place.

Megan blinked, wondering who he was and what he was doing in a sleepy town like Minoa, Nevada.

Lifting a hand, he slung his thumb through a belt loop at his waist and glanced around the room. Two tables sat vacant, but Megan hadn't cleared them yet. His gaze brushed past, screeched to a halt, then rushed back to settle on her. She felt the weight of his gaze like a ten-ton sledge. A frisson of awareness swept over her. She couldn't move. Her feet felt as if they were stapled to the floor.

He walked toward her with a masculine swagger that told her he knew where he was going and exactly what he wanted once he got there.

Megan ducked her head and pretended to organize a panel of hot water glasses, fresh out of the dishwasher. From her peripheral vision, she watched the man sit on a bar stool directly opposite her and lean his elbows on the clean counter.

"Good morning." She placed a menu and a glass of ice water in front of him.

"Morning, ma'am." His deep voice sounded like rolling thunder.

She didn't meet his eyes but could feel his gaze boring a hole in the side of her head.

A rattle of dishes caused her to turn just as Caleb and June ran past the bar stools in a game of chase. With fast reflexes, Megan snatched both of her kids by the arms and pulled them back behind the counter.

"Hey, you two little imps. What did I tell you about running through the restaurant?" she scolded in a low voice.

"Sorry, Mommy." June gazed at her with wide, uncertain eyes. A smattering of freckles stood out across the bridge of her button nose, her blond ponytail bouncing.

"Yeah, we're sorry, Mom," Caleb crowed happily. So much like his father. Too agreeable to really understand that he'd done anything wrong. He just went along with his big sister.

As Megan smoothed Caleb's rumpled T-shirt and flyaway hair, she gazed at her children's sweet faces. Thinking how much they each looked like their daddy. Thinking this was no place to raise two active little kids. During the school week, she had them in an after-school program. But nights and weekends, they were here with her. She spent so little time with them as it was that she wanted them near her whenever possible, even if she had to keep working. Besides, she couldn't afford a lot of child care. Not on her tight budget. Thank goodness most of her customers were friends and neighbors who didn't mind seeing her kids in the diner now and then.

Megan hugged her children close, breathing deeply of their warm skin. A wave of unconditional love swept over her. Just what she needed to dissolve her frazzled nerves.

"How about if I take you to the park for an hour later this afternoon to play?" she said.

"You're not too busy?" June asked.

Megan shook her head. "I'll make time. We'll go once the lunch rush settles down a bit. I'm sure Connie can handle things for a while."

"You know I can. You guys go and have a little fun," Connie said as she whisked by, carrying a tray of food for table number five.

"That would be fun," June said.

"Yeah, and we can play kick ball," Caleb said. He drew back his leg and kicked the air for emphasis.

"Okay. We'll do it. But aren't you tired now?" Megan asked.

She'd gotten both kids up at five that morning. As always, they hadn't uttered a single complaint. Just rubbed their sleepy eyes and trundled out to the truck in their jammies. They'd changed into their street clothes later that morning. Because she practically lived at the restaurant, Megan had created a homey environment for them in the back office, where they could have some privacy to watch TV, color or sleep. But sometimes, they got restless. Like today.

"Nope, not a smidgen," June replied, mimicking a phrase her father had often used.

Megan fought off a rush of guilt. Her kids should be outside, running in the tall grass and swinging in the park. They were just children, after all. This situation wasn't their fault. It wasn't anyone's fault. But they still had to cope.

"You will be tired, my little June bug." Megan brushed her index finger across the tip of her daughter's nose.

After they'd played in the park, she knew they'd both collapse on the cot she'd set up in the back office. Just in time for another rush of customers wanting their dinner. In the meantime, it was more than difficult to keep an eye on two wriggly children while she was working.

"Why don't you go in the back and watch TV for a while?" she suggested.

"I don't want to," June said.

"Do you want to help me instead?" she asked them, her voice enticing.

"Sure," Caleb chirped with a ready nod of his head.

Megan swept a jagged thatch of hair back from her son's forehead. "I've got two bags of garbage sitting beside the back door. If you work together, you can carry them outside and throw them into the dump. And after you've had your lunch, I told Frank to save a slice of fresh banana cream pie for each of you."

"Yum!" Caleb gave a little hop and clapped his chubby hands.

June smiled wide, showing a missing tooth in front. "Okay, Mommy. We'll do it."

And off they went.

"Cute kids," the handsome stranger at the counter said.

Megan glanced his way, feeling pleased, but suddenly self-conscious that he'd over-heard her entire conversation. "Thanks."

Swiveling on her flat, practical heels, she faced him. Her gaze dipped to the menu, which he hadn't touched.

"Thanks, but I don't need it." He shook his head, a subtle smile curving the corners of his full mouth.

She slid the menu into the holder at the side of the cash register. Gripping her note-pad and pen, she forced herself to meet his dazzling blue eyes.

"So what'll it be, then?" she asked.

He flashed a magnetic grin. Wow! He had gorgeous blue eyes. Intelligent yet soft, with smile lines at the corners. His sun-bronzed skin told her he liked being outdoors.

"Steak and eggs, cooked medium rare and over easy. Fire potatoes, two griddle cakes and whole wheat toast with plenty of straw-berry jam."

Yep, his order was completely masculine, just like him. Coasting on autopilot, she slid a dish of prepackaged jams close to his hand. She jotted some notes, trying to get his order down before her muddled brain forgot everything.

He gave an infectious laugh. "You sure write fast. Have you got it all? I can repeat it, if you like."

"Nope, I've got it. Anything to drink?" she asked, forcing herself not to look up.

"A tall glass of orange juice, please."

"Coming right up." She swiveled around and snapped his order up for Frank.

Forcing herself to keep working, she fled to the kitchen refrigerator to pour him some juice. She returned and had just set the glass in front of him when little Caleb came running in from the alleyway out back. He tugged on her apron and spoke in a shrill voice.

"Hurry, Mommy! Fire! Outside," the boy cried.

The handsome man sitting at the counter jerked his head up, his eyes widening.

Wiping her hands on her apron, Megan scurried after her son and muttered under her breath. "What could make this day any crazier?"

* * *

The moment Jared Marshall heard the word
fire, he was out of his seat. Without a backward glance, he followed Megan Rocklin
down the hallway leading to the back door.

Yes, he knew the woman's name. He was
new in town, but Tim Wixler, his assistant
fire management officer, had told him what
she looked like. Though the description he'd
been given didn't do Megan justice. No, not
at all.

Jared had come here specifically to speak
to her about a catering job, but he'd never
expected her to be so pretty and petite. She
had a stubborn chin, pert nose, long straw-
berry blond hair and warm brown eyes. No,
not really brown, but rather a golden amber.
With reddish flecks in the center. Yeah, he'd
noticed, in spite of her reticence to look at
him. And in spite of his desire not to notice.

As he passed through the narrow hallway,
he snatched a fire extinguisher off the wall.
The screen door clapped closed behind him as
he stepped out into the alley. Megan's daughter was screaming and jumping up and down
in absolute panic. Looking at his sister, the
little boy followed suit and burst into tears.
When Megan saw the flames licking above
the top of a metal garbage can, she gasped.

"Where's the lid? Can anyone find the lid? I've got to snuff the fire out," she cried, searching through the rows of garbage cans lining the outer building.

Without hesitation, Jared pulled the ring on the extinguisher, aimed the nozzle at the trash can and depressed the trigger. A whoosh of white foam hit the flames. Within seconds, the fire was out.

The girl stopped screaming and the boy stopped crying. The two kids huddled next to their mom's legs and sniffled. The poor little things were scared, and Jared thought that was good. After this experience, he doubted they'd ever play with matches.

"Oh, thank you." Megan spoke with relief, one hand cradling Caleb's head next to her thigh, her other hand clasped to her chest.

"You're welcome." Jared nodded, conscious of the cook, waitress and several customers from the restaurant coming outside to see what the commotion was about. Their eyes were filled with helpless frustration.

"I wonder what caused the fire," Megan said.

Jared glanced around the narrow alley. His experienced gaze took in the variety of garbage cans, plastic black bags and a litter of cigarette butts lying in the dirt by the back door.

He pointed at the butts. "I suspect that's your culprit. Someone could have tossed a hot cigarette into the garbage can and it ignited."

"Of course. But how did you know what to do?" Megan asked. "You were so quick to react. It would have taken me several more minutes to remember the fire extinguisher. In all these years, I've never had to use it."

He shrugged. "It's what I do. I'm glad to help."

She tilted her head. "What do you mean? What do you do?"

"I'm the new fire management officer at the Forest Service office in town. Normally I'd be wearing my Forest Service uniform, but I'm off duty today."

Her face flushed a deep red. A cloud of doubt veiled her expressive eyes. "Oh. You're a firefighter."

It wasn't a question. She said it as if it was something to be abhorred.

"So, you're the new FMO." Connie stepped forward and shook his hand. "We haven't met yet, but you work with my husband, Tim Wixler."

Jared smiled with recognition. "Sure. Tim's a great guy. I'm glad to have him as my assistant FMO."

"But you fight wildfires," Megan said again, as though she couldn't believe it.

He nodded. "Yes, or rather, I used to. Now, I just organize the people and equipment for fighting fires on the Minoa National Forest. Although I'm also the newest member of the voluntary fire department here in town." He smiled, a frisson of pride filling his chest. In spite of suffering a painful divorce last year, he still loved his work. It's all that had kept him sane after his ex-wife left him for another man.

"Well, I appreciate the help. Your meal is on the house," Megan said.

"Nah, you don't need to do that," he countered.

"Sure I do. It's my way of saying thank-you."

He stepped forward and offered her his hand. "My name's Jared Marshall."

"I'm Megan Rocklin." She took his hand in a tentative grip, but she didn't smile.

"I'm glad to meet you, Mrs. Rocklin."

She nodded. Without another word, she turned her shoulder on him and looked at the husky man wearing a chef's hat. The cook. Jared had seen the guy back in the kitchen, preparing breakfast.

"Frank, I'm afraid you may have caused this fire. Can you be more careful with your cigarette butts in the future? I've got insurance, but I'd sure hate to have the place burn to the ground." Her voice sounded gentle but stern.

Frank's round face flushed red. "I…I'm sorry, Megan. I thought my cigarette was out. I didn't mean to cause any harm."

The poor guy looked profoundly apologetic. The little girl named June took his hand and leaned against his side in a silent show of support.

Megan relented, a smile of understanding creasing her face as she hugged the big man in a warm gesture of forgiveness. "I know you didn't mean any harm. Just please be careful in the future. Or better yet, now is a great time to quit smoking altogether."

"Maybe you're right," Frank said, his bushy brows pulled down in a thoughtful frown.

Jared liked this woman. Liked the way she treated her kids and her employees. She seemed to really care about them. And after what he'd been through with his ex-wife and her selfish demands, that meant a lot.

"Well, no harm done," Jared said.

All eyes riveted on him. No one said a word. They looked at him as if he'd grown horns on top of his head. And suddenly, he felt out of place. As if he didn't belong. Not yet, anyway. But he planned to change that over time. He loved the quiet camaraderie of this small town, the slower pace, the beautiful stands of timber covering the Sierra Nevada Mountains. This was his kind of place, and he was staying. He'd thought putting out the fire might win him a few new friends. So, why did he feel as if he was a leper trying to infect everyone? Maybe it was because they didn't know him yet. He was a stranger, after all.

"Okay, the show is over, folks. Let's get back to business." Megan opened the screen door and urged her children, Frank and other people inside.

Jared held back, deciding to watch the fire for a while longer, to ensure it was really out.

Megan beckoned to him. "You don't need to worry. I'll keep an eye on it."

"If you've got a bucket, I'd feel better to dump some water on it, just to make sure it doesn't flare up again."

"Yes, I can do that. Why don't you come inside and Connie will get your meal for you?"

She stood, holding the screen door open, her stubborn chin lifting a notch higher in the air. Her beautiful eyes didn't quite meet his. They seemed cold and remote, now. Not quite hostile, but almost. He felt her disapproval like a living thing and wondered what was wrong. What had he done? Since he'd mentioned that he fought wildfires for a living, she'd changed toward him, and he didn't understand why. Most people loved firefighters. They were considered heroes. A profession little boys dreamed about becoming part of when they grew up.

"Actually, I was hoping to talk with you for a few minutes," he said.

She pursed her lips. "About what?"

"I have a job offer for you."

She let go of the screen door and it clapped closed. She tucked a curl of reddish-gold hair back behind her ear, looking beautiful and vulnerable.

She indicated the diner, her brows lifting in an irritated frown. "I have a job already. I own this restaurant."

"I know, but this would be right up your alley and shouldn't interfere with your café. I need a caterer. Someone who can prepare meals for the crews of men and women during the summer fire season coming up."

She snorted. "I've got two kids. I can't flitter around, traveling from state to state to provide food to firefighters."

"You wouldn't have to. I just need you for the fires we get in our own mountains, which shouldn't be too many. Tim Wixler told me you've done it before."

Her mouth rounded and she hesitated. "Yes, but not anymore. I'm afraid it wouldn't work for me now."

"You sure? I heard that you own a mobile kitchen and lots of tables and chairs."

"Yes, that's true, but I've advertised all of my equipment for sale."

"Then you know what the work entails. Since you're the only restaurant in town, I wanted to give you first dibs on the job. Reno is eighty miles away, so I thought I'd ask the locals first."

Her frown stayed firmly in place, and he hurried on, wondering why he felt desperate for her to accept. "It's just for the summer and it wouldn't be dangerous. You'd be serving meals up at the fire camp, which would be far away from the fire."

She gave a derogatory snort. "Yeah, it's safe. With all those big airplanes, bulldozers and pumper trucks driving around the place. No thanks."

Hmm. Maybe she did have something against firefighters after all.

"It's good money. We pay top dollar." He didn't know why he kept enticing her. She'd said no, but he'd noticed how shorthanded she was in the restaurant. That could be because someone had called in sick, or because she couldn't afford to hire more people. Whatever the cause, he felt certain that she needed the extra income. So why wouldn't she accept his offer?

"I'm not really staffed to cater meals to a bunch of unruly firefighters anymore," she said.

Unruly firefighters? He was one of them. And from what he'd been told, her husband had been one, too. So why the animosity?

"I could help you get set up," he offered. "If you can provide the equipment, workforce and prepare the food, I can provide you with the Cubitainers. I've even got two extra power generators I could let you borrow."

Because she'd done this kind of work before, Megan should already know that Cubitainers were clear, square plastic containers for putting juice, milk and water in. They were stackable and easy to transport.

"I'd make it as painless as possible," Jared continued. "All you and your people have to do is cook and serve the food to the crews for an occasional fire."

Okay, he was trying too hard. And yet, he felt as though his future happiness depended on her acceptance. A crazy notion if ever he'd had one.

She shook her head. "No, I'm sorry. I can't."

He flashed her a smile, determined not to be upset by her rebuttal. She must have her reasons for declining, and he couldn't fault her for it. "Okay, I understand. If you change your mind in the next few days, just say the word. I won't be going into Reno to approach other possible vendors there for another week or so. You've got time to change your mind."

"I won't change my mind."

"Well, just in case." He reached inside his shirt pocket and pulled out one of the new business cards his office manager had made up for him two weeks ago when he'd first arrived in town. Handing the card over to Megan, he noticed how her hand trembled as she took it. She barely glanced at it before sliding it into the pocket of her apron.

"Thanks." She turned and went inside, leaving him to follow at his own pace.

She returned with a bucket of water a few minutes later. While she resumed her work in the restaurant, he dumped the water into the rusty garbage can. He checked on the fire one last time, satisfied that it was really out. Then, he went inside for his meal. It was delicious and he finished it way too soon. And when he tried to pay his bill, Megan refused to accept any money. Instead, he left a twenty-dollar bill tucked beneath his plate when she wasn't looking. A very tidy tip he thought she'd earned.

Walking out into the sunshine, he climbed into his blue pickup truck and drove home. But he couldn't help wishing that Megan Rocklin had accepted the catering job.

Chapter Two

"You should accept his offer," Connie said.

"Whose offer?" Megan sat at the counter in the restaurant, refilling the salt and pepper shakers. Frank was in the kitchen, getting ready for the dinner hour. The kids were finally taking a nap in the back office. For a few brief minutes, Megan had not a single customer to wait on. But she knew that would soon change.

"Jared's offer. You should cater meals to the fire crews this summer."

Yes, Megan knew who Connie was talking about. But she'd rather avoid the discussion. She'd been stunned when she'd discovered who Jared was and what he wanted. After Blaine's death, she figured she'd never cater meals to the firefighters again. And frankly, she wasn't mentally prepared to think about it now.

"No way. You know I've vowed to keep my distance from the firefighters. It's bad enough that many of my friends are hotshots I have to worry about. I don't want to go up on the mountain with them."

"But you haven't sold your mobile kitchen yet. You still have all the equipment you need."

Megan barely glanced up as she rolled a fork, knife and spoon in a paper napkin, taped it closed, then placed it into the basket they used to serve their customers. "That'll change as soon as I find a buyer."

Connie caught a drip of pancake syrup as she refilled the smaller decanters from a gallon jug. "Look, Megan. You've had that mobile kitchen up for sale for months now, and no one has expressed any interest in buying it. So why not use it for something good? Being around them doesn't mean you'll fall in love with another firefighter—though there'd be nothing wrong with that. You've just got to feed them."

True, but that wouldn't sway Megan. Being in the fire camp would be too much of a reminder of all that she'd already lost. "Give me boring and safe any day of the week."

Connie frowned. "I don't know how you can limit love that way. When you fall for someone, you fall. Your heart doesn't care what he does for a living. I don't think you can stop it from happening just because their work might be dangerous."

"That might be true, but I'm no longer willing to take the chance," Megan insisted.

"I hope that's not true. It sounds kind of sad," Connie said.

Megan snorted. "Not half as sad as trying to explain to my two children that their daddy won't be coming home because he was killed in the line of duty."

Connie pushed aside the syrup bottles and reached out to hug Megan. "I know, sweetie. You've been through a lot and I'm so sorry. But please don't give up on love. You're a wonderful person and have so much to offer some good guy. One day, you're gonna meet someone special and have a long, wonderful life together."

Megan just nodded, not really believing she could ever be so blessed to experience that kind of exquisite love a second time.

"Catering meals for the firefighters would still be great for your business," Connie said.

That was true.

"But what would I do with Caleb and June? They'll soon be out of school for the summer and needing even more attention."

"You could take them to child care."

"Yes, but not overnight. I spend so little quality time with them as it is. When they're not in school, I hate for them to be out of my sight if it's not absolutely necessary."

"So, take them with you. It'll be fun for them," Connie said.

Megan arched one brow. "You mean up on the mountain?"

"Sure. They're well behaved and will stay close by while you deliver the food. They'll look at it as an adventure. You don't need to stay overnight and serve the meals. You can hire reliable people to do that for you."

Megan couldn't argue with that. Connie made a valid point. She liked for her kids to see her working because they usually pitched in and helped. Megan knew that was also a great way of teaching children to have a good work ethic. "But we don't have enough people to run the restaurant and also go up on the mountain to feed all the fire crews. We're talking about hundreds of hungry men and women."

Connie shrugged, looking undeterred. "So, hire more people to help you out. You've done it before. Summer is your busy time. Lots of hungry tourists coming through town. It also means that many high school students are out looking for jobs. In a dinky town this size, they're kind of limited on employment options. I have no doubt they'd love to chop lettuce and serve food for minimum wage. And the school lunch cooks are out of work, too. They'd love a summer job. If we have a forest fire, you can be the shuttle to drive the food up to the base camp every day. And June and Caleb can ride along with you. You get to spend time with them, and they'd have a good time. Problem solved."

It sounded so simple when Connie put it that way.

"We could definitely use the money," she said.

But catering meals meant she'd have to work around the firefighters. No doubt she'd end up seeing Jared Marshall now and then, too. And for some reason, being around the enigmatic FMO made her feel nervous and jittery inside. She didn't understand why, but she realized she liked the guy already.

"I'll help you," Connie said.

"So will I," Frank called from the kitchen.

Megan's face flushed with heat when she realized Frank had been listening in. She thought she was crazy to even consider taking on the job. But maybe Connie was right. The thought of earning enough money to bring her bills current was an enticement she couldn't resist. And if she refused to do the work this year, Jared might not ask her again next year. She'd be passed over while he hired some big restaurant out of Reno. It wouldn't be often. The surrounding mountains usually only had one or two fires each year. And she could always sell the mobile kitchen later on, after fire season was over with. But it wouldn't be wise for her to pass up this golden opportunity.

"Look, honey, I know you're still upset about losing Blaine, but this catering job is safe. And all you've got to do is say yes," Connie said.

An abrasive laugh slipped from Megan's throat. "It's not safe no matter what you say, but I guess the fire camp should be harmless enough."

"That's right," Connie said. "And now that I've convinced you on this one thing, maybe you'll also listen to me regarding your love life. It's time to start dating again. You need a night out for a change."

"Ha! I own the only restaurant in town and there's no movie theater. So what am I going to do on a date? Drive out and look at the lake?" Megan pursed her lips.

"It sounds kind of romantic to me. Cuddling up to a handsome man who has eyes just for you," Connie said.

Megan didn't agree. Going on a date was as appealing to her as a case of the measles.

The bell over the door tinkled as a man and woman came inside. Connie hurried to wait on them, calling over her shoulder. "Think it over. Tim said he knows someone he'd like to set you up with. He told me to ask you about it."

"Who is it?" Megan asked.

Connie shrugged as she pulled her notepad out of the pocket in her apron. "Beats me. Tim just said he's a nice, steady guy."

Great. Steady and boring. But that was what Megan needed in her life. No more excitement. No more wildfires to make her anxious at night when she should be sleeping.

Connie provided their customers with menus and two glasses of ice water. In her heart, Megan knew dating another man wouldn't work. She didn't want to jump into another relationship. Not as long as she had June and Caleb to think about.

Still, she did consider the possibilities. A lot, in fact. As she served food and closed up the diner later that night, her thoughts trailed back to Jared Marshall. His smile alone was enough to make her heart beat faster.

After locking the front door, Frank walked with her and the sleepy children out to the parking lot and said goodbye. Standing beneath the dim glow of a streetlight, Megan let the frigid night air cool her work-flushed face. A heavy doubt blanketed her. A constant companion she couldn't seem to banish from her heart and mind.

As she buckled her two kids into their seats and closed the door, a chilling breeze smelling of rain swirled around her. She walked to the driver's side, thinking that the catering job wouldn't be too bad. It would be a lot of hard work, but that never frightened her. Loving and then losing someone to a wildfire was a different matter entirely. It absolutely terrified her. And she couldn't go through that again. No, not ever.

The microwave buzzed, letting Jared know his dinner was ready. Having just gotten home after a long day at work, he changed into his old blue jeans and a worn T-shirt. Switching off the light in his bedroom, he padded barefoot through the dark living room to the cheery lights of the kitchen. Reaching for a hot pad, he opened the microwave and slid his dinner onto the kitchen table. A frozen spaghetti-and-meatballs concoction from a cardboard container. Nothing fancy, and nothing like the meal he'd had at Megan's diner the day before, but it'd fill up his rumbling stomach.

The doorbell rang and he jerked his head around. He glanced at the clock on the wall. Nine twenty-eight. Who could be calling at this late hour?

Walking into the living room, he clicked on the porch light. Opening the door, he looked out. Megan Rocklin stood in front of him, wearing a light jacket and a worried frown.

"Mrs. Rocklin! Come in," he said.

A whoosh of air rushed out of his lungs, and his senses kicked into overdrive. Wow! This was unexpected. Even with a mountain of work, he couldn't stop thinking about her throughout the day. He'd planned on going back to her restaurant, to ask her about the catering job one more time, but decided to let it drop. Now he was beyond startled to find her on his doorstep. In a town this size, he wasn't surprised that she knew where he lived, but what was she doing here?

"No, I can't." She tossed a desperate look toward the street, as if she wanted to escape.

Beneath the glimmer of the porch light, she fidgeted, looking anxious. He caught sight of her old pickup truck parked in front of his house. Through the windows, he could just make out the tops of her two children's heads, snuggled together in sleep. A sweet feeling rushed over him. He liked these kids and their mother.

"Did you just get off work at the restaurant?" he asked.

"Yeah, we're on our way home now."

He gazed at her face, delicate and pale in the dim night air. Lines of fatigue circled her expressive brown eyes. And in that moment, he realized how difficult life must be for her, running a business and raising two young children on her own.

"What can I do for you?" he asked. If only she'd agree to cater meals to the firefighters, he could bring her some lucrative work that might allow her to hire some more help.

She looked casual in faded jeans. Her blue tennis shoes matched the neck of her soft sweater almost exactly. In the restaurant, she'd worn her reddish-blond hair tied back in a ponytail. Just now, it lay in flowing waves across her shoulders, and he thought she must have pulled it loose and brushed it out before leaving work.

"I'm sorry to bother you at home so late at night, but this is the first chance I've had to get away from the diner," she said, her face flushing a delightful shade of pink.

He caught her fragrant scent and took several deep inhales. He couldn't help contrasting her relaxed attire to the formal dress suits his ex-wife had worn all the time. After college, Sharon had wanted him to go into banking, like her father. Jared had almost done it, too. After all, his parents had died and he'd wanted to please his new wife and her family. But wearing uncomfortable suits and sitting in an office all day long didn't appeal to Jared. He loved his forestry work and being outdoors. Too late, he had realized that he and his wife had wanted different things from life.

"It's no problem. What can I help you with?" He smiled, genuinely pleased to see her again.

She glanced at the dark street, then ducked her head, clenching her delicate hands together like a lifeline. She cleared her voice and swallowed before speaking. "I was just wondering if the catering job is still available."

He released a silent breath of relief, more than glad that he had put off going into Reno to ask another business to do the job. "Yes, it is. Are you interested?"

She hesitated several moments. "Yes, I think I am."

He stepped forward, his fingers tightening around the doorknob. "Great. I'm glad to hear that."

"But first, I've got a few questions."

He lifted a hand in the air. "Of course. Ask anything. If I don't know the answer, I'll find out the information for you."

She took a deep breath, as though she were about to plunge headfirst into an icy pool of water. "How much notice will I get when you need me to feed the fire crews?"

"About twenty-four hours. Is that enough?"

She nodded. "Yes, I think so. How many people will I need to plan on feeding?"

"Around four hundred. Some big fires require feeding two thousand people, but if we get to that point, I'll bring in some additional caterers. Although you'll also need to feed about fifty people at the spike camps. Those are remote camps which are mostly for smoke jumpers and hotshot crews. You won't need to go into the spike camp to serve the meals but rather prepare the food so we can fly it in by helicopter."

Another nod. "Yes, I know what a spike camp is."

His mouth dropped open. "That's right. Your husband was a firefighter, too."

"Yes."

He barely caught the word, she spoke so quietly.

"Would you be able to feed that many people?" he asked.

"Yes, I think I can manage that number just fine."

"Good. I've got a watering trough we can fill with ice and then just dump the cans of soda pop and bottled water into it for people to grab and run. But you'll need to keep a large coffeepot hot and ready twenty-four hours a day," he said.

"That sounds fine. I've got several giant coffee pots we can use. Will you need me to provide the ice?"

He nodded. "Yes, please. And I suggest you hire two or three more cooks to help you prepare the food. Will that be a problem?"

She finally met his eyes. "No, I'm planning to speak with some people I know tomorrow afternoon. Since it's seasonal work and only if we get a fire nearby, I think they'll come out of retirement to help me. I also know of two school cooks who are out of work for the summer. I think they'll jump at the chance for this kind of job. I'll alternate their schedules, so they don't get too worn out with the long hours. And then, I'm hoping to make a trip into Reno next week, to buy some additional equipment. Once I've got everything ready, I thought you could come over to check it out."

Impressive. He much preferred hiring an experienced caterer like Megan. She obviously knew what she was doing, but yes, he would want to check it out. "That would be fine. It sounds like you've already thought this through."

"I have. But—" she swallowed again "—I just want to make sure my food crew won't be anywhere near the forest fire."

He hesitated. Obviously, he wouldn't put her or her people in harm's way. And yet, she seemed to be overly worried about it. And for some odd reason, he felt a protective impulse come over him. To reassure her. To keep her safe.

"No, you won't be working close to the fire. The camps are usually situated in a safe zone. I'll ensure your protection. I can promise you that."

She released an audible breath, and it finally dawned on him that though most people would want to be assured of the same thing, Megan's reasons stemmed from having her husband die in a fire. And he couldn't blame her.

"Mrs. Rocklin, I can assure you that no harm will come to you or your people. Safety comes first with me. We can replace buildings and trees, but no one should ever be injured or die in a forest fire." And he meant what he said. Deep inside, he knew he'd do whatever it took to keep his word.

A slight smile curved her lips, and she stepped back on the front porch. "I'm glad to hear that. And please, call me Megan."

He smiled too, beyond relieved to have a caterer set in place. This was his first assignment as an FMO, and he wanted to do a good job. Contracting people to provide food, bulldozers, drop planes and pumper trucks was a large part of his work. He felt better having this item settled.

They discussed her fee and a few other details. As she stepped down off the porch and headed toward the sidewalk, he accompanied her to her truck.

"I can bring the contract by your restaurant in a day or two for you to sign," he said.

Zipping her jacket up to her throat, she met his gaze. "That would be fine. And thank you. I won't let you down."

He smiled. "I have no doubt that's true."

She opened the door to her truck. And as he watched her climb inside, flip on the headlights and drive away, he felt surprisingly happy inside. A strange notion that made him question why. And though he hated to admit it, he knew the answer. He wanted to see more of Megan Rocklin. And that knowledge left him feeling both a little frightened and excited all at once.

Chapter Three

"Mommy, that man's here."

Megan looked up. Caleb stood in the doorway of the laundry room in their house.

"What man?" Down on her hands and knees, Megan wrung out a dripping rag into the mop bucket. She blew a long tendril of hair out of her face and glanced toward the threshold again. Jared Marshall stood there, tall and imposing. Little Caleb stared up at the man, a look of hero worship filling his eyes.

"Oh!" Megan's mouth dropped open and her eyes went wide. She almost groaned out loud, thinking this day couldn't get much worse. Why did this gorgeous man have to catch her mopping up a mess from the leaky washing machine?

Dressed in his Forest Service uniform, Jared held several white papers in his big hands. In a rush, Megan sat back with a thump, taking in the bronze shield pinned to the left front pocket of his drab olive green shirt. He looked so official. So imposing.

Bracing her hands against the floor, she pushed herself to her feet, a knot of tension tightening at the back of her neck.

"Hi, Jared. I didn't expect to see you today." She dropped the rag into the bucket, noticing that her wet fingers were wrinkled like prunes.

His gaze swept across the room. He observed the washing machine pulled away from the wall, the tools resting on top of the dryer and the sheen of water still covering the damp floor.

She felt nervous and out of sorts having this man in her home. Her house wasn't fancy, but it was normally clean and comfortable. So, why did he have to show up just now, when everything was in a mess? And why did she care what Jared Marshall thought about where she lived anyway?

He chuckled, the low sound sending a shiver up her spine. "I'm sorry to interrupt, but I guess we keep surprising each other."

"Yeah, we sure do. You caught me at a bad time. The washing machine sprang a leak." Her voice sounded unnaturally high to her ears.

She turned and moved the bucket out of the middle of the floor. Facing him, she lifted her chin, trying to retain a bit of dignity.

Pretending not to notice her predicament, Jared waved the papers in the air. "I brought over the contract for you to sign. I took it over to the restaurant, but they told me it was your day off. I figured you wouldn't mind if I stopped by."

Her breath whooshed from her lungs. "Of course not. I only go into the diner on Mondays if they get swamped by customers. It's usually our slow day. I was trying to catch up on some laundry, but it didn't work out quite as I'd planned."

She took a step, her tennis shoes squeaking against the tile floor.

She indicated the towels and a load of soggy clothes still sitting inside the washing machine drum, half-filled with water. They were waiting for a spin cycle that wouldn't come, and Megan dreaded rinsing the clothes before wringing them out by hand. With everything else she had to do today, she didn't need this problem to cope with. She wanted her laundry clean and put away.

"Jared can fix the washer, Mommy," Caleb said with confidence.

Both Jared and Megan snapped their heads in the boy's direction, looking surprised. Jared closed his mouth and his gaze zeroed in on the washing machine. June joined Caleb, watching the scene with wary eyes.

"I pulled it out away from the wall, so I could get at the problem," Megan said.

But the truth was, she didn't have any idea how to fix the machine. Megan had used the wrench to shut off the water, but not before she'd been doused by the spray. She pushed a limp strand of hair back behind her ear, highly conscious that she must look horrible. No makeup. Her hair a mess. Dressed in worn blue jeans and a ratty sweatshirt.

"I have no idea how to fix the leak," she confessed.

And the drowsy little town of Minoa didn't include a plumber. Folks usually dealt with problems like this on their own. It was expensive to bring an expert in from out of town. Blaine had always handled these situations for them, which was just one more reason she missed him. She'd been about ready to call Tim Wixler, to see if he might be able to come over after he got off work. Now she didn't want to ask for Jared's help, but she sure could use it.

"Looks like the washing machine made quite a mess," Jared said.

"It did. Water was all over the place. Huh, Mommy?" Caleb scrunched up his nose as he gestured at the walls and floor.

Megan dried her hands on an old towel and heaved a disgruntled sigh. "Yes, I was just cleaning it up."

"My dad always fixed the washer," June said in a slightly defensive tone.

Jared quirked one brow in an endearing smile. "He did, huh? I'll bet he was very handy at fixing things. Do you mind if I take a look?"

June didn't respond. She just studied him, her eyes narrowed with suspicion.

"Please do. And thank you." Megan stepped back to let him through, tugging on her children's arms to get them out of the way.

Right now, she didn't care that Jared was a wildfire fighter. She'd be grateful just to have her washing machine back in commission. Besides the added expense of buying a new machine, she didn't have time to drive into Reno to shop for one right now. If necessary, she could do it when she went into the city to buy the extra equipment she needed to cater meals to the firefighters, but that wasn't her preference. Her budget was stretched too tight already.

"Why don't you read through this while I see what I can do?" Jared handed her the contract and scrunched his tall frame into the narrow alcove behind the washer so he could inspect the hoses connecting the machine to the faucet.

Megan took her kids into the kitchen, where they all sat at the table and she pored over the contract. There were two copies, and she assumed one was for her. She'd just signed on the bottom line when Jared came in wiping his damp hands on a towel.

Caleb popped out of his seat and stood wriggling with anticipation. June folded her arms and scowled at the man.

"You don't happen to have any hose washers, by chance?" Jared asked.

Megan cocked her head to one side. "What do you mean?"

He held out his hand. On his calloused palm rested a little black washer that was split in two. "This kind of washer. It seals the connection between the faucet and the hose. This one is split, which is what I believe caused your leak."

She crinkled her nose in a grimace. "It was

more like a geyser. And yes, I use those kinds of washers on my garden hoses."

He nodded. "Yes, that's right. Do you have any extras lying around?"

She stood and pulled open a drawer filled with a variety of junk. Tape, string, paper clips. A catchall drawer where she stashed odds and ends. She snatched out a small package she'd put there last summer and handed him a washer.

He flashed a satisfied grin. "I'll have it fixed in a jiffy."

"See? I told you so. Jared can fix anything," Caleb crowed with victory.

June didn't say a word. Just sat there with a frown tugging at her brow. Megan figured the girl was feeling territorial because a strange man was in her house. A man that wasn't her daddy.

Megan and the kids followed Jared into the laundry room, craning their necks to watch him work.

"Can you show me how to fix it? Then I'll know what to do the next time this happens," Megan said.

"Sure. Come here." Jared waved her over.

The children stood beside the dryer while Megan squeezed in against the wall and Jared placed the washer inside the hose opening.

Standing this close to the man, she caught his clean, spicy scent and gulped in a shaky breath.

He screwed the connection onto the faucet and tightened it down. As he worked, his arm brushed against hers, sending currents of warmth and energy zinging up her arm.

She stepped away quickly, her face heating up. "You think that's it?"

"We'll know in a moment," he said.

Wrapping a towel around the connection, in case it sprayed the room again, he turned the water back on with several quick twists of his wrist. The hose pulsed twice as it filled with water, then held strong. Jared tossed the towel aside, then moved the washing machine back into its position beside the wall.

"That's it. You're all set," he said.

"Wow! You made it look so easy." Megan gazed at the washing machine with awe.

"Yeah, I think you got the hard part of cleaning up the mess."

She chuckled. "Thank you so much. I really appreciate this."

"Yay! Jared did it." Caleb jumped up and down.

But June just scowled.

Jared reached out and ruffled Caleb's

thatch of unruly hair. He smiled wide at the two children. "It was my pleasure."

A liquid feeling of warmth washed over Megan. Her children were starved for a man's affection. Even June. And Jared was so likable. Her kids needed their daddy, but fate had been cruel to them all. They still grieved for Blaine, but with this handsome stranger standing in her home, Megan couldn't help thinking about the possibilities. She missed having a man around the house. The deep laughter as he played with her children. The brute strength to fix a broken pipe. The soft hugs and assurance when she was feeling lonely or sad.

"Now we have to celebrate and say thank-you to Jared with some ice cream and cookies," Caleb announced.

Megan released a shuddering breath. "Yes, of course." She didn't want to serve ice cream to the FMO and, in spite of him fixing her washing machine, she wished he hadn't come to her home. But how could she say no? Her children didn't understand her aversion to firefighters and that she didn't want Jared to linger. They only knew their daddy was a hotshot. And that Jared was a nice man that had helped them out twice.

"Actually, I've got to get back to the office," Jared said.

"But you gotta stay for cookies. They're homemade. You just gotta," Caleb howled.

"My mother makes the best cookies in town," June said, folding her arms and lifting her chin higher in the air. It was almost a challenge. As if Jared would offend them if he didn't eat one of their cookies.

Megan refused to meet Jared's eyes. A conflict as old as time waged a war inside her mind. The desperation to protect her family fought against her desire to be near this amazing man. She couldn't tell him to leave, but neither could she ask him to stay. The choice was his alone.

"Okay, I'll try at least one," Jared said.

"Yippee," Caleb whooped.

The boy tugged on Jared's hand, pulling him into the kitchen. Megan followed, letting her daughter help her as she got out a tub of vanilla ice cream, four bowls and a plastic scoop. Jared sat in a chair to wait while Caleb placed the cookie jar in the middle of the table. Within minutes, they were all munching on fresh cookies and spooning ice cream into their mouths.

Megan nibbled her treat in silence. One thought pounded her brain. She'd already signed the catering contract. It was too late to take it back. Her copy sat on the table.

Jared had folded his copy and slid it into his back pocket. And now more than ever, she questioned her judgment in agreeing to cater meals to the firefighters. It would only serve as a constant reminder of her lost love. But honestly, she didn't have the courage to ask for the contract back.

Jared wished he hadn't come here. He should have waited until tomorrow when he could have returned to the restaurant to give Megan the catering contract to sign. Because now he'd caught a tiny glimpse of what it felt like to have a family of his own. A wife and children that needed him as much as he needed them. All the years he'd been married to Sharon, she'd put off having children. And out of respect for her feelings, he hadn't pushed her. But not having kids was one of his biggest regrets.

Now he needed to get out of here. Before he remembered how lonely he was. But Megan must be lonely, too. He'd seen the pictures in her living room, hanging on the walls and standing on the top of the piano. Pictures of Megan with her kids and a man. Her husband. If the wide smiles were any indicator of happiness, he figured she'd loved the guy more than anything else. And Jared couldn't help wishing there was just one person in this world that loved him like that. That there was one woman who missed him when he was gone and couldn't wait to see him again.

He ate his ice cream too fast and immediately regretted it. Pressing his fingers against his forehead, he clenched his eyes tightly shut as pain throbbed through the top of his head.

"What's the matter, Jared?" Caleb asked.

"Brain freeze," he spoke low and tight.

At least the pain took his mind off how wonderful it was to sit at this table and enjoy the laughter of two sweet kids and their overly quiet mother.

"You ate your ice cream too fast," June said.

"Mom says to eat slowly, so your food will digest properly," Caleb said.

Jared almost laughed, thinking what a proper, wonderful mother Megan was to her two children. The kind of woman he wished he'd met and married back when he'd first started his career with the Forest Service. She hadn't known how to handle her broken-down washing machine, but she'd tried. She worked hard at the restaurant, seeming to pull her load without complaint. She did what had to be done. And he respected her for that. But he knew it couldn't be easy on her.

"I'll remember that the next time." He gritted out the words in a strangled voice.

When the pain in his head eased, he stood and placed his bowl and spoon in the sink. "Well, I better get going."

He looked at Megan, noticing her pale face and wounded eyes.

"Hey! Maybe Jared can fix our broken swing, too," Caleb said.

June looked up, her mouth pursed with annoyance. Jared tensed, getting the impression she didn't like him horning in on the chores her father used to do.

Jared met Megan's eyes. He wanted to help out, but he also felt uncertain about his role in this family's life right now. He wasn't really a friend, and yet he wanted to be.

"No, Jared's got to get back to work, kids." Megan chewed her bottom lip, looking worried and stressed.

"Ah," Caleb grumbled. "I haven't been able to swing for the longest time. Can't he take a look, Mom? Please?"

Interesting how the boy asked his mother's permission, as though naturally assuming Jared would be willing to do the task. And once more, he realized how much this family was missing their dad. It didn't help that Caleb was looking at him with such deep desperation that it tweaked his heart. Jared couldn't say no. But little June had misgivings. He could tell from the way she sat quietly looking at him. As though she couldn't make up her mind whether she liked him or not. And that softened his heart, because she was so young and innocent. Because she missed her dad.

"I can take a quick look," Jared said.

Okay, not smart. Hadn't he just been itching to get out of there? He needed to go before this little family squeezed its way any further into his heart.

Before it was too late.

"Well, if you've got the time. The swing's out back. The toolbox is in the garage. The kids will show you the way," Megan said.

"Sure! Come on. I'll take you there." Caleb hopped off his chair and headed for the back door.

June followed behind, seeming hesitant to accept Jared's help. "When it works, it's the best swing ever. My dad made it for us out of an old tire, but it needs a new rope."

"Yeah, you're gonna love it," Caleb chimed in.

Jared nodded his head and followed the two kids outside. Before he knew what was happening, Caleb had slid his hand into his, talking nonstop.

"My dad put in this grass for us last summer. He wanted us to have a nice place to play. He threw the baseball to me and showed me how to wrestle," the boy said.

Jared listened without saying much. Along the way, they passed a semitruck and the mobile kitchen, both parked beside the garage. The portable kitchen was a white structure with window cutouts for serving food. Without a word, Jared sized it up, thinking it should work out fine for the catering job. When Megan was ready, he'd return to inspect her other equipment, just to make sure she had what she needed to do the job. But so far, he wasn't overly concerned.

"Someday I'm gonna get me a dog. I just got to convince Mom," Caleb continued in a happy voice.

"You do, huh?" Jared didn't know what else to say.

"Yep. My dad was gonna get me one, but then he died. Now Mom says we're too busy for a dog. She says it'd have to stay home all the time while we're at the restaurant working."

"It'd poop all over the place anyway," June said.

"But I'd clean up after it. Besides, it'd be good to have a watchdog to protect us in case some bad guys try to get into our house," Caleb said.

Jared's heart constricted with compassion. He thought about how difficult it must have been for these two children to lose the father they loved. And he was glad to do something to help them out.

"Bad guys aren't gonna break into our house," June said, but she didn't sound convinced.

"Well, they might," Caleb argued.

June just shook her head.

"Daddy bought a new rope for our swing, but he got killed before he could put it up," the girl informed Jared in a matter-of-fact voice.

She showed him where the yellow rope lay coiled on the workbench in the garage. After inspecting the black rubber tire, Jared quickly set up a ladder and a sawhorse to hold the weight of the tire as he hoisted it over the sturdy tree branch. He then shimmied up the ladder and tied a knot in the rope to hold it tight. A gust of warm air blasted him in the face, and he thought about the dry winter they'd had and the coming fire season. He had no doubt he'd be seeing more of Megan over the coming months, and that caused a flutter to fill his chest.

Caleb was the first to try out the swing. As

Jared pushed the little boy through the air, his laughter was infectious. Even June smiled. Jared never knew that making two kids happy could bring him so much joy, as well.

Glancing up, he caught Megan watching him from the kitchen window. Heat flushed the tips of his ears. Her face looked quiet and pale. As if she didn't approve of him being here. He knew this had been her husband's job. He should still be here, pushing Caleb and June on the swing. Not him. Not a stranger. These weren't his children. This wasn't his wife and family. Tension knotted the muscles at the base of Jared's neck. It was best not to get too attached to these youngsters or their beautiful mother.

As he continued to look at Megan, he saw a slight frown tugging her delicate brow, and her eyes filled with misgivings. Tim Wixler had told Jared what a happy couple Megan and her husband had been. Now she was cautious and guarded.

A flurry of emotion overwhelmed him. He really needed to go. He said his goodbyes and suffered through a heartwarming hug of gratitude from Caleb. Even June thanked him. But Jared didn't go inside the house to tell Megan farewell. And as he got into his Forest Service truck and drove away, he reminded himself that he didn't want another woman in his life. His ex-wife had left him for another man. She'd found happiness with someone else. Someone that wasn't him. Jared had no desire to put his heart at risk a second time.

Megan was a contractor for catering meals to the firefighters and nothing more. He had put out a fire at her restaurant, fixed her washing machine and the tire swing. That was enough.

At least, that's what he had to keep telling himself to make sure his heart stayed safe.

Chapter Four

Megan walked up the front steps of Connie and Tim Wixler's tan stucco house. Lifting her head, she caught the tangy aroma of barbecue in the air. The afternoon breeze fluttered over her, teasing wisps of hair around her face. Although it was unseasonably warm, the air held a slight chill and she was glad she'd worn a sweater.

Connie had arranged for a babysitter for Caleb and June. A teenage girl from down the street had come over to stay with the two kids. Megan thought it was kind of nice to have a night away from her children. She couldn't remember the last time. On the one hand, she felt guilty for not spending more time with them. After all, they were her main priority now that Blain was gone. But on the other hand, she longed to feel carefree and happy again. And she wondered if that was even possible anymore.

She knocked on the door but didn't wait for someone to answer. Having been here dozens of times over the past ten years, she turned the knob and stepped inside.

"Hello! Anyone here?" she called to the empty living room.

Voices and laughter came from out in the backyard. The house smelled of boiled eggs and potatoes, and she figured Connie must have made her delicious potato salad.

She walked into the kitchen, noticing the clutter of dishes, plastic wrap and food items spread across the countertops. No doubt Connie had been cooking up a storm. But why make so much food for just three people?

Through the screen door, Megan caught sight of Tim standing in front of the propane barbecue. Brian Dandrige, the superintendent of the Minoa Hotshot crew, and his girlfriend, Gayle, stood beside the table. Sean Nash, the crew boss of the hotshots, and his fiancé, Tessa, were chatting with Connie over a bowl of chips, dip and finger foods. Old friends, every one. Other than seeing them at the restaurant now and then, Megan hadn't mingled with them much since Blaine's death. Not because they hadn't called or come by to visit her. She just hadn't wanted to socialize much with other people.

Megan felt suddenly edgy and anxious. She hadn't realized dinner at Connie's house would include some of Blaine's old coworkers. She thought it would be a quiet evening, just the three of them.

Taking a deep breath, Megan tried to settle her nerves. Blaine had been gone almost a year, and it was time for her to get out and be around others. But it wasn't easy. In a way, she felt disloyal to Blaine for moving on and living while he had died.

Stepping over to the screen door, she pushed it open and went outside.

"Hi, Megan! It's so good to see you," Gayle called.

"Hi there!" Megan smiled and waved, doing her best impression of pretending she wanted to be here.

"Howdy, Megan. How do you take your steak?" Tim asked.

"Medium well. Where do you want me to put this?" She lifted the bowl of pasta salad she'd brought with her, hoping she had enough for this large crowd.

"Over there." Tim pointed his tongs at the picnic table, set up beneath the shade of a tall wisteria tree in full bloom. The afternoon breeze wafted the sweet aroma of flowers to her.

Breathing deeply, Megan turned and froze. Across the expanse of green grass, Jared Marshall stood beside the table holding a can of soda pop in one hand. The afternoon sun gleamed against his dark blond hair. He was dressed casually in a pair of navy blue slacks and a white polo shirt that fit his muscular arms and chest to perfection.

Her gaze locked with his for several pounding moments. His dazzling blue eyes crinkled at the corners, and she realized he was just as confused as she was. Maybe Tim had thought this a good way for Jared to get to know the crew leadership in an informal setting. Brian and Sean were year-round employees. The rest of the hotshot crew was seasonal, working during the summer months and into the early autumn.

But in a rush, Megan realized what was going on. This gathering wasn't just for the hotshots to get to know their new FMO. Her mind quickly did the math. Eight people were here. Four couples. Each of them were romantically involved, except for her and Jared. This was a setup, pure and simple. Connie and Tim had been pushing her for months to let them fix her up on a blind date, but

Megan had refused. Obviously, Connie had decided to ignore her and had paired her with the handsome fire management officer. A pseudo blind date. Under false pretenses. Because Connie knew Megan would never have agreed to come otherwise.

"Megan, I'm so glad you're here. You can help me with the baked beans." Connie engulfed her in a warm hug.

"You've been very devious," Megan whispered.

"Yes, but you'll forgive me. You always do. And since you're here, try to have a teensy bit of fun." Connie spoke low, for her ears alone. Then the woman drew back and smiled as she whisked the bowl of pasta salad out of Megan's hands. "I'll take this for you. It looks delicious."

Connie turned toward the table. "Jared, would you please get Megan a drink?"

"Sure," came his hesitant reply. His gaze shifted to her flushed face, and he jerked one shoulder. "What would you like?"

"Something diet," Megan said.

He brushed past her as he reached inside the cooler chest. He rattled around in the ice for a moment before pulling out a diet cola. After he popped the tab, he handed the can over with a smile. They drew together close enough to chat without including everyone else in their conversation.

"It looks like we both got ambushed," he said.

A warm, fluid feeling washed over her. He would have had to be blind not to realize that Connie had paired them up for the evening. Obviously he hadn't been in on the surprise either, but Megan didn't know if he resented it or not. And her face heated with embarrassment.

"You didn't know there would be other people here tonight, either?" she asked to confirm.

He shook his head, an uncomfortable smile curving the corners of his handsome mouth. "Nope. I thought I would be their only guest. I think we got played by a couple of masterminds."

She took a sip of her soda, the carbonation burning her throat as she swallowed. "Yeah, some matchmakers. But I fear it's mostly Connie's doing. She's not pleased until everyone is happily married off. She just doesn't understand the word *no*. I'm so sorry about this."

"Don't be. It's not your fault."

And she knew it wasn't Jared's fault, either. She just wasn't ready to start dating again.

Especially not someone who worked in such a dangerous profession. Nor was she prepared to bring a man into her small family. Even having Jared fix the swing in her backyard had upset little June. Megan knew it wasn't because June didn't like him, but because he wasn't the girl's father. Caleb was young and loving toward everyone, but Megan didn't want to push June too fast. The girl wasn't ready for another daddy in her life. Neither was Megan ready for another husband. It was that simple.

Or was it? Megan sighed. Maybe she should at least try to find happiness with another man. And yet, she couldn't seem to let go of Blaine. They'd been college sweethearts, and she'd loved her husband for so long that she didn't know how to stop now that he was gone. Honestly, the thought of dating another man made her feel disloyal to the love she'd shared with him.

"I figure we have two choices this evening," Jared said in a soft voice. "We can leave right now, or we can stick it out and try to have some fun."

"There's a third option," Megan said, trying not to sound too angry.

He quirked one brow. "And what's that?"

"We could strangle Connie and Tim and then flee to South America."

Jared laughed, a rich baritone that seemed to soothe her jangled nerves. "I'm afraid the cops would catch us for sure. Are you okay with spending some serious time in jail?"

She shook her head. "No, I've got children waiting at home. We better stick with option number two."

"I'm game if you are."

"Okay," she conceded, trying to be a good sport. But it wasn't easy.

She stooped down and petted Connie's dog. An old basset hound named Sam.

"My kids keep asking me for a dog," she said.

"Yeah, Caleb told me. Are you going to get them one?"

She shook her head. "Maybe someday. Right now, we're never at home. And the poor animal couldn't come with us to the restaurant. It would violate the health codes. But Caleb keeps asking anyway."

"I've been thinking about getting a dog myself."

She crinkled her nose. "Really? They are lots of hard work. I keep telling Caleb that, but he won't listen. He informed me the other day that kids are supposed to have a dog. That he needs to learn responsibility. And what better way to do that than by taking care of a new puppy?"

Jared chuckled. "Don't worry. I'm pretty sure Caleb and June will grow up normal and well-adjusted even without a dog."

"I hope so." She laughed, trying to sound happy. But inside, she was screaming. She already liked this man too much. Spending more time as his date tonight would only make matters worse. But it looked as if she didn't have a choice right now. Not unless she wanted to be rude.

"Would you like some chips and salsa?" he asked, indicating the colorful bowls Connie had set out for her guests.

"Sure."

He accompanied her over to the table nearby. His voice was deep and warm. He bumped against her arm and the feel of his fingers against her bare skin made her entire body thrum with reaction. Megan glanced up in time to see Tessa playfully swat Sean on the shoulder. He said something that made her laugh. In response, Sean gave her a hug and kissed her lightly on the cheek. Tessa snuggled in close against his chest. They were engaged to be married in December and seemed so natural and happy together. And Megan envied the love they shared.

"They're a cute couple, aren't they?" Jared said, noticing her gaze.

"Yes, they are. They deserve to be happy."

"They definitely do. Where are your kids tonight?" Jared asked.

"Home with a babysitter."

"It must be nice to have a night off."

"It is," she said.

She looked up, meeting his eyes. He stood close enough for her to feel his warmth. To catch his scent. She stared at him, mesmerized. Frozen in time. For several quiet moments, nothing existed in the world except him. An insane notion, considering they were standing in Connie's backyard and surrounded by lots of other people. Then, Megan came to her senses and stepped away.

But she was still speechless. *Think!* What should she say? Something to appear ordinary and unaffected. To regain her composure and fight off this emotional assault.

"How long have you been here in Minoa?" she asked.

There. That was good. Something normal and logical.

"Not quite a month. This is my first job as a fire management officer." He picked up a tortilla chip, scooped up some salsa and popped it into his mouth.

"What did you do before this assignment?"

"I was the superintendent of a hotshot crew in Arizona. Tim and I used to work together back in the day. We've been friends for a long time, so I was happy to accept this job," he said.

She wasn't surprised. The world of wildfire fighting could be quite small. "So, I guess you're pretty good at fighting wildfires."

He shrugged. "I like to think so, but I'm cautious, too. I don't take any unnecessary risks that might endanger my crew. Their safety always comes first with me."

Blaine had been cautious, too, but it hadn't stopped a firestorm from rolling right over the top of him with very little notice. When the forest supervisor had brought her the news of her husband's death, he'd told her that Blaine hadn't suffered much. Which Megan knew was code for he'd died in a fiery inferno that had killed him very fast.

Tears burned the backs of her eyes, and she looked away so Jared wouldn't see. Shaking her head, she tried not to think about that now.

"Did you know my husband?" she asked.

"What was his name again?"

"Blaine Rocklin. Before coming to Nevada, he worked on a hotshot crew in Colorado. But over the years, he worked on quite a few fires in Arizona and Idaho."

Jared shook his head. "I'm sorry, but I don't think I ever met him."

At the mention of Blaine, warning bells jangled inside her head, and she stepped farther away. Jared was exactly the kind of man she'd vowed never to love. And yet, a sudden jolt of longing speared her. She felt so comfortable being with him. It was kind of nice to be a couple again. To feel as if she belonged. Especially when Jared was so easy to talk to. But knowing what he did for a living, she told herself it would never work. She had to think about her kids. To think about their future. No more sitting at home worrying that she might receive a dreaded phone call. Or the Forest Service supervisor might show up on her doorstep to bring her the horrifying news that the man she loved was badly hurt or killed in the line of duty. Nope, her heart couldn't take that risk. Not ever again.

"Time for charades. Each couple is going to be a team," Connie called to the group after they'd finished eating their steaks and fresh strawberry pie.

Jared blinked, his mind racing. Couples meant he'd be with Megan again. There wasn't any way he could politely get out of it. But charades? He'd never played games with his ex-wife before. In college, she'd been fun-loving and he'd enjoyed being with her, but after they'd married, Sharon had changed. She'd come from a wealthy family. In school, she'd let her hair down and done whatever she wanted. But once they were married, it seemed that earning money was the most important thing to her. She'd never approved of his decision to work for the Forest Service. He didn't earn enough, nor did he receive the kind of attention in his career that she thought he deserved. And yet, he'd loved his work. And she'd come to resent him for it.

Now Jared glanced at Megan, trying to read her body language. She sat beside him at the picnic table, her eyes wide and luminous. Nothing to indicate she minded teaming up with him in a game of charades. And yet, he saw a twinge of reservation in her. The tense set of her slender shoulders. The way she wouldn't quite meet his eyes.

She was as wary of him as he was of her.

She tucked a loose strand of hair back behind her ear, then smoothed a hand over the front of her flower-print scarf. Feminine and lovely. Even wearing faded blue jeans, she looked dainty. He thought of the way she ran her business, raised her two children and dealt with the day-to-day problems of life. She was a real girlie girl with a lot of spunk he admired. But seeing her again had punched him in the chest. He wanted so much to be good friends with her, but wasn't sure he dared. She didn't appear to be interested in romance, and neither was he, but he didn't want her to get the wrong idea.

"Come on, gather around." Connie waved to get everyone's attention.

They left the picnic table and assembled on the patio. As the group sat in the yard chairs, Megan perched herself along the lip of blocks edging the cold fire pit. Not knowing what else to do, Jared sat beside her and waited.

Connie produced a hat and an egg timer. She handed each person eight slips of paper and a pencil, then explained the rules to the game. "Write down your ideas and we'll put them inside the hat. The team that guesses the most words wins a nice prize—dinner and a movie in Reno."

The group oohed and ahed as they nodded their understanding. Jared glanced over at Sean and Tessa. They sat close together, with Sean's arm lying casually across Tessa's shoulders. Brian and Gayle were cuddled up much the same. But Jared wasn't fooled by their easy manners. Competition would undoubtedly be fierce tonight. And he'd be happy to lose. He wanted the prize to go to another couple.

"What if we draw our own words?" Brian asked.

"Then, you'll have an advantage, but it'll still be difficult to act them out," Connie said.

Jared took his pieces of paper, trying to think of words to jot down. Megan shifted beside him on the stone hearth, and he realized she must be as nervous as he was. For the rest of the couples, winning the prize would be fun and something to look forward to. For Megan and Jared, it was a conundrum. If they won, they'd have to make arrangements to drive into Reno and share another date together. It was good incentive for him to lose on purpose, but he knew that wouldn't be much fun for Megan. And for some odd reason, he hated the thought of disappointing her.

"Are you up for this?" he asked her in a low voice.

"Sure." Her voice wobbled, and he thought she was trying hard to be agreeable, just like him.

"It's difficult to think up words," Gayle said.

"Not for me." Brian folded his slips of paper and tossed them into the hat before showing a smug smile.

A few more minutes, and everyone finished writing out their words. Gayle giggled in anticipation.

"Tim and I are the oldest, so we'll go first," Connie said.

"That means Sean and Tessa are last. They're the youngest," Tim quipped with a laugh.

Megan didn't say anything. Neither did Jared. He just pasted a smile on his face and nodded. What else could he do? But he couldn't help feeling protective of Megan. Conflicting emotions thrummed inside him. He'd be a callous heel if he didn't consider her feelings, but he wasn't interested in a movie and dinner in Reno. No way, no how.

After stirring the slips of paper, Connie held out the hat to Tim. He reached inside and opened their first word, showing it to his wife. They whispered among themselves for a few seconds, then began. Connie held her hands together, as though she were reading a book. Then, they all laughed at the way portly Tim tried to act like a wriggling worm. It didn't take long for everyone to guess the word *bookworm*.

The group fell into a routine, with each couple demonstrating funny actions and the rest of the teams trying to guess the words. Within a few minutes, they were all snorting, chuckling, shouting out answers and having a great time. Finally, it was Jared and Megan's turn.

They stood as Connie held out the hat. Jared jutted his chin, indicating that Megan should draw their word. She did so and unfolded the scrap of paper for them both to see at once.

Milk fat.

Megan groaned. "This one is hard."

The other couples snickered.

Jared leaned near and whispered for her ears alone. "You want to take the word *milk,* and I'll take *fat*?"

Megan nodded, a long strand of her hair tickling his nose. He took a deep inhale, breathing in her delicate scent of springtime, sweet and warm.

Standing in the open, Megan signaled that she was ready to begin by lifting one finger.

"First word," Tessa said.

Megan nodded and held up her hands, as though she were pouring a glass of milk. Jared watched her every move, understanding perfectly. But she had to convey her actions to the other couples, too.

"Pour," Tim shouted.

"Glass," Gayle said.

"Drink," Sean said.

Moving quickly, Megan shook her head each time, then switched her tactics. Crouching down, she moved her hands as if she were milking a cow. The entire group laughed, including Jared. He watched her with amazement. She was beautiful and fun and wonderful.

"Cow," Connie said.

"Squeeze," Tessa said.

"Udders," Tim said.

The group roared. Megan narrowed her eyes on Tim and shook her head, but she was giggling, too. This game was definitely an interesting way for Jared to get to know his coworkers.

"Milk," Brian finally said.

Megan clapped her hands and nodded before stepping back. It was Jared's turn. He held out two fingers.

"Second word," Tessa said.

Jared nodded, then bent his knees, puffed out his cheeks, and held out his arms as though he had an enormous belly.

"Fat!" Tim yelled.

Jared nodded. Obviously Tim was good at this game.

"Milk fat," Connie called.

"Yes," both Jared and Megan cried simultaneously.

They made a good team. She bumped against him in laughter, and he wrapped his arm around her, giving her a light hug. It was a spontaneous gesture he didn't think about until it was too late.

She hugged him back, her eyes meeting his. They were having fun together, and there was no denying the attraction. But that evaporated in a flash. The realization of what she'd done dawned in Megan's expressive eyes. They both jerked back in surprise and turned away. The tips of Jared's ears felt hot with embarrassment.

A few moments later, Jared joined her at the hearth, standing instead of sitting. He couldn't help liking this woman. The way she tried so hard to be kind. Her sense of humor, in spite of being forced into a blind date with him. But he'd promised himself he wouldn't get sucked into a relationship for a very long time, if ever. And now, he was in trouble. Because tonight had given him a glimpse of what it could be like with a woman like Megan. And he pitied her husband for dying. For not being able to be here with her anymore.

They didn't speak much for the rest of the evening, which went by in a haze. Brian and Gayle won the prize. And honestly, Jared was beyond relieved. It took all the pressure off.

Darkness covered the yard, with a gentle breeze blowing in the scent of lilacs. And when Megan walked outside with the rest of the guests to go home, her truck wouldn't start. Knowing Jared and Tim would take care of the problem, Sean and Brian took their sweethearts home. Jared and Tim checked the engine to Megan's truck, but it was almost impossible to see anything in the dark. Tim got a couple of flashlights out of his garage, but it didn't help much. Megan's frustration showed in her desolate expression.

"First my washing machine, now my truck. I can't believe this is happening now. The last thing I need is car trouble. I seem to be having a bit of bad breaks lately," she said with a wan smile.

"Why don't I plan to open the restaurant tomorrow for you?" Connie offered. "Then you won't have to worry about it. I don't want you and the kids walking over there alone so early in the morning."

Standing in the graveled driveway, Megan

gave the woman a squeeze of gratitude. "I'd sure appreciate that. Thank you. I'll make it up to you with some time off later in the week. I promise."

"It's no problem," Connie reassured her.

"Jared, since you're headed that way, would you mind giving Megan a ride home?" Tim asked.

Hmm. If Jared didn't know better, he might think that Connie and Tim had planned this situation on purpose. His common sense told him that wasn't the case, but after the evening of surprises they'd had, he wouldn't put it past Tim to pull a spark plug or two in order to stop the engine from working.

"Sure, I'd be happy to," Jared said.

He spoke the words with misgivings. As he looked at Megan's rusty old truck, he figured it had seen much better days. He wanted to get her home safely, but then what? She needed wheels to get around town with her kids. And to drive up onto the mountain to cater meals to the firefighters. The last thing he wanted was for her to be stranded midway on the mountain while the fire crews went hungry. He didn't want to worry about her, but she was one of his contractors now. She needed a reliable vehicle that would get her from point *A* to point *B* without any trouble.

So, what could he do about it?

"Jared and I will see about repairs for you first thing tomorrow morning. Don't you worry about a thing," Tim told Megan.

"Thanks. I'd appreciate that."

Jared opened the passenger door to his truck and waited while she climbed inside. Closing the door, he walked around to the driver's seat. He'd inserted the key, started the engine and flipped on the headlights before she spoke again.

"I'm sorry about this." Her voice sounded soft and sincere.

He stared out the windshield as he pulled onto the narrow road. "It's no problem. Car troubles are a part of life. And I live just a couple of blocks away from you, so we're in the same neighborhood."

She glanced his way. "Yes, I know."

Of course she did. She'd come over to see him last week, when she'd agreed to work as a caterer for him. He had to remind himself that her husband used to work for the Minoa Hotshots. She'd been a firefighter's wife, just like his ex-wife. And yet, she seemed to fit in so well with the other hotshots. Without resentment. Without hating everything about small towns. Without longing for the large shopping centers and bright lights of a big city. Instead, he got the vibe that Megan was well-adjusted to living here in Minoa. That she actually liked being here. If only Sharon had been the same way, their marriage might have worked.

"Have you lived here long?" he asked.

She nodded, gripping the armrest with whitened knuckles. No doubt she was still upset about her truck. "Yes, eight years. We moved here just after June was born."

"Do you like it here?" He decreased his speed as he turned down Main Street.

She flashed a smile. "Oh, yes. It's a sweet community. Perfect for raising a young family. I wouldn't live anywhere else now. I grew up in Elko, Nevada, but my husband grew up here. That's how we got the restaurant. His father died five years ago and left the diner to us. Since I'd graduated from culinary school, I loved to cook. It seemed a perfect fit. A great way to do what I love. Then, four years ago, we bought the mobile kitchen, to cater meals to the firefighters. While Blaine worked his job as a hotshot, I ran the diner and catering business. But we never thought it would end so soon."

Her voice cracked and so did his heart. He held the steering wheel with both hands. "I'm sorry you lost him."

"Thanks," she said very quietly.

And that was that. They didn't speak again until they arrived at her house. The air seemed to fill up with a lot of unspoken words. They both had past loves and broken hearts. Hopes and dreams that had been dashed to smithereens. Vanquished yearnings that kept rattling around and making a lot of noise in their minds.

He pulled into her driveway and killed the engine, then hopped out and hurried around to open her door. He helped her down, then walked with her up the dark sidewalk to her front doorstep. The cool night air smelled of rain. Another lightning storm that had the potential to start a forest fire in the mountains. Except for being set up on a blind date by Connie and Tim, it'd been a perfect evening. Despite his misgivings, he had enjoyed himself tremendously.

"I know neither of us planned it this way, but I had a lot of fun tonight," he said.

"Yeah, me too. Thanks."

"You're welcome."

She stood close, and he gazed into her soft brown eyes. A hypnotic force seemed to pull him nearer, until his gaze lowered to her lips.

The porch light came on and the door jerked open.

"Hi, Mommy!" Caleb called.

June bulldozed her way past her brother and stood there with her arms crossed and a disapproving frown curving her mouth. "Hey, are you gonna kiss my mom?"

"No! Of course not." Heat flooded Jared's face.

"June, don't be rude," Megan said.

"Yuck! I'd never kiss a girl. You might get a disease." Caleb stuck out his tongue in disgust.

"You won't get a disease," June said.

"Will, too," Caleb replied.

Jared couldn't help laughing. If he had two little kids, he'd want them to be just like Caleb and June. But the situation was anything but comfortable.

"Sorry, Mrs. Rocklin." The babysitter pulled the children back inside the house and closed the door.

Jared breathed a sigh of relief, but he couldn't help chuckling as he jerked his thumb toward the house. "Looks like you've got two little watchdogs."

The children had hopped up on the couch and had their noses pressed against the glass windowpane as they peered out at them.

"Yes, they're a bit overly protective of me. I'm sorry about that." She turned her back on the kids and gave Jared a half smile, her eyes filled with unease.

He looked away. "They're good kids."

"Yes, they are." She hesitated. "Thanks again."

He nodded. "You're welcome."

They looked at each other, each assessing the situation for what it was. Her eyes mirrored his concern. Neither one of them wanted to be hurt again. For that reason alone, they couldn't take this relationship any further.

"Well, I'll say good-night." He slipped his hands into his pockets.

"Good night." She waved as he stepped down off the porch and sauntered toward his truck.

He got inside and fired up the vehicle, but waited until she went inside before he backed out and drove away. It'd been a long time since he'd been out on a date and driven a woman home. A long time since he'd thought about kissing someone good-night. And the sad truth was that he wished he had met a woman like Megan about ten years earlier.

Chapter Five

The following morning, Megan sat on the sofa in her living room tying her shoelaces when the doorbell rang.

"I'll get it," Caleb cried as he dashed for the door.

Standing on tiptoes, the boy had trouble negotiating the dead bolt. June, who was much taller, helped him turn the lock. The door whooshed open to reveal Jared standing there with a wide smile.

"Good morning," he said.

"Jared!" Caleb launched himself at the man.

As usual, June held back, a bit withdrawn.

Jared scooped the boy up and swung him around. Caleb's laughter filled the air like musical wind chimes. Watching them together, a lump rose in Megan's throat. She remembered her husband doing this exact same thing.

Still holding her son, Jared smiled at June. "How are you, sweetheart?"

She sat on the edge of a chair and folded her arms, lifting her chin in a haughty stare. "I'm fine, thank you. But what are you doing here?"

"June! Don't be rude," Megan said, though she couldn't help wondering the same thing. She felt like her daughter. Filled with trepidation. She hadn't seen Caleb this happy since before his daddy's death. Her son was young and might soon lose most of his memories of his father, but June was older. And like Megan, would never forget.

Jared shrugged, seeming undeterred by the girl's glower. "I was hoping to speak to your mom for a few minutes, if that's okay."

June didn't respond.

Megan stood and waited for Caleb to settle down. In spite of knowing that Connie was opening the restaurant for her that morning, Megan had woken up early. Worried and too nervous to sleep the night before, she had dressed and gotten the kids their breakfast, planning to walk with them the six blocks to Main Street. She needed to speak with Grant Metcalf, the owner of the only gas station in town. Hopefully, he'd be able to haul her old truck into his garage for repairs as soon as possible. And hopefully, the work wouldn't cost her an arm and a leg.

"Jared, look! I've got a loose tooth." Caleb gritted his teeth and pressed against a wobbly tooth in the front.

"Yeah, that's great, buddy," Jared said. "How's the swing working out?"

"Great! You wanna come out back and see it? When I pump my legs hard, I can go so high." Caleb lifted his arms over his head to emphasize his words.

Jared glanced Megan's way. "Maybe tomorrow. Right now, I need to speak with your mom, and then I've got to get into work."

Megan's heart gave a maddening thump, then sped up into double time. Her son liked this man. A lot. And so did she.

Looking out the living room window, she saw a strange truck parked in her driveway. Jared owned a blue pickup truck, but this one was different. At first glance, she thought it must be his work vehicle. It was Forest Service green, but had no markings to indicate that it was a government-owned vehicle.

"What are you doing here so early in the morning?" she asked.

He set Caleb down and jerked his chin toward the driveway. "I've got a business matter I need to discuss with you. Can I speak with you outside for a few minutes?"

Wondering what on earth he wanted, she stepped out on the porch with him and called over her shoulder to the children. "You kids stay inside. June, help your brother find his shoes and put them on."

"Ah, I wanna come with," Caleb groaned.

Megan gave him a stern look. She didn't want her children around when she told Jared that he should stop coming over here. "Finish your breakfast and get your shoes on, son. I'll be right back."

She closed the door firmly against the boy's protests and went outside with Jared. He led her to the driveway, finally stopping beside the green vehicle. Gleaming water droplets clung to the front fender, as though it had been freshly washed. Jared pressed his fingers against the passenger door. As usual, he looked dashing in his Forest Service uniform. He stood there, tall and handsome, and flashed that devastating smile that made her stomach swirl with butterflies.

"Good morning," he said.

"Good morning. What's up?" Okay, not too harsh, but blunt enough to let him know that she wanted to get down to business.

He tapped the front fender with his finger. "Since you're without wheels right now, I thought maybe I could help you out."

Confusion fogged her brain. "What do you mean?"

"I thought you could use this truck."

She stared at the vehicle as if it was a three-headed monster. "I don't understand."

He shrugged his powerful shoulders, a smile widening his sun-bronzed features. He'd slicked his hair back with a bit of gel, and his jaw was blunt and determined. "It's a loan. To use while you're working with me. You can drive it here in town and also when you cater meals to the fire crews up in the mountains this summer. Whatever you need. You can return it once the fire season is over in the fall."

Her mouth dropped open, and she had to consciously close it. "But I'll have my own vehicle repaired soon. I can use it to drive up in the mountains."

He shook his head, his voice light but insistent. "No, your truck is too old and unreliable. I don't want you and your people broken down somewhere on a deserted road where there isn't any cell phone service to call for help. I told you when you agreed to be one of my contractors that I'd provide some of the equipment you'll need for your work. And that includes this newer truck. Besides, it'll save you wear and tear on your vehicle."

She blinked in shock. "Who does this one belong to?"

"Me. I bought it three months ago at a surplus sale. At the time, I didn't really need it, but it was in excellent condition and such a good price that I didn't want to let it go. The Forest Service is the original owner, so it's been maintained very well. It's got a trailer hitch, so you can pull your supplies behind and you shouldn't have any problems with the engine."

She took a step back. "Oh, no. I can't accept this."

He met her eyes, looking surprised. "Why not?"

"I don't accept handouts."

His brow crinkled with disapproval. "It's not a handout, Megan. It's a tool. A truck. So that you can do your work to feed the fire crews. That's all."

Hmm. She wanted to believe him but couldn't help feeling suspicious. It was more than just a truck. It was him inserting his life into hers and helping her out even though she hadn't asked for it. His continued generosity touched her, but she wouldn't accept charity. Not as long as she could find a way to help herself.

"How about if I rent it from you?" she asked.

He opened his mouth, then closed it, as though he wanted to argue, but realized it was futile. "Okay, but just enough to cover the mileage. Say twenty dollars a month?"

She snorted. "How about a hundred dollars a month, along with parts and service?"

He folded his arms, making the fabric of his sleeves tighten around his big biceps. "Make it fifty and an occasional home-cooked meal, and we've got a deal."

Oh, boy. His terms would mean that he'd be coming over to her house now and then to have dinner with her and the kids. Laughing, joking, having fun. Becoming good friends. And she couldn't let that happen.

"I'll agree to seventy-five," she said, omitting anything about fixing him dinner.

He stood before her, his legs spread slightly. Unfolding his arms, he rested his hands on his lean hips. Solid and tenacious. But she could be stubborn, too. On the one hand, she wanted to accept his offer. She'd be crazy not to. She'd already spent a sleepless night wondering how to pay for major repairs on her old junker truck. Wondering how she was going to get her kids back and forth to school and the restaurant, much less haul food up on the mountain. But on the other hand, Jared was being too generous. There to bail her out of trouble as he'd done with the washing machine and the ride home the previous night. And it'd be crazy to have him over to the house for supper with the kids. Kind of like jumping from the pan into the fire.

He shook his head, the sunlight gleaming against his dark blond hair. "Nope. Fifty dollars a month or no deal."

So he'd called her bluff. They stood there looking at each other in a standoff, and neither of them spoke for several pounding moments. She couldn't deny the urge to accept all that he offered. It'd be so easy to say yes. To give in and make life easier on herself. But it was an illusion. She'd pay a heavy price later on. She couldn't get any closer to him. Even as friends. No, not again. She just couldn't. She opened her mouth to tell him so, but the words wouldn't come out.

"Agreed, but you'll have to eat your home-cooked meals over at the restaurant," she finally said. "As a general rule, I only have Sunday and Monday nights off, so I'm not usually here at home during the dinner hour."

Of course, she could invite him over on her

nights off, but she didn't say that. It was better not to offer that option to him.

Placing the key in her hand, he flashed a smile so bright that she had to swallow.

"Agreed," he said. "And we've already had Grant Metcalf tow your truck over to his garage for service."

"We?" she said.

"Yes, Tim and me. He thinks the alternator's gone out. If that's the case, Grant said he'll have to order parts, which could take several weeks before the repairs are done."

She shook her head, feeling dazed. He'd made this matter so simple for her. She hadn't had to do a single thing. "You've already spoken to Grant about my truck?"

He jerked one shoulder. "Yeah, Tim and I took care of it for you early this morning. I thought it might help you out since you've got the kids to deal with and all."

"I was going to see Grant now," she said.

"Actually, Tim made the first call to ask the mechanic to come over and tow your truck back to his garage and take a look at the engine," he said. "I just followed up to find out what he thought the problem was. Tim says the guy's good. And seems that he is, because Grant said it can be fixed but it will take time."

Oh. So Jared hadn't acted completely on his own. Like all the other hotshots, he was just looking out for Blaine's widow. And she shouldn't be surprised. Even though Jared had never met him, her husband had been one of their own. And they had been a big, happy family. And while Grant wasn't a hotshot, he'd gone to high school with Blaine, and they'd been close friends for a lot of years. She couldn't really fault the guys for taking care of the family Blaine had left behind.

Not when she needed them so much.

And it was obvious that, more and more, Jared seemed to fit right in with the hotshots. He kept rescuing her from one problem after the next. And she could get used to this. To become complacent and comfortable. But she knew security was a mirage. A facade that didn't last. She had to stay sharp and independent so that she could ensure her kids were taken care of. But her service in her church congregation had taught her that gratitude was also important. And right now, she was very grateful.

"Thank you. You've made everything so easy for me," she said.

She felt as if she needed to repay him somehow. The monthly stipend they'd agreed upon for her use of his truck seemed insufficient. Maybe she could let the kids take him a plate of homemade cookies later that night. Or have a standing order that he ate at the restaurant for free. And yet, she wanted so much more. A loving husband to come home to each night. Someone to share her fears and joys with.

No! She must harness those kinds of thoughts. There could be no more. Not with this man. Not ever.

"It's my pleasure." He glanced at his wristwatch. "And now I better get into the office."

He turned and headed down the sidewalk.

"Wait!" she called after him.

He paused, pivoting on his boot heels. "Yes?"

"How will you get to the Forest Service office? After all, you drove your truck here and are leaving it behind for me to use."

"I'll walk, of course. It isn't far."

No, in a community this size, walking wasn't so difficult. Unless you were driving to one of the ranches outside of town, everything was pretty close together. But she didn't feel right about leaving him afoot.

"If you'll give me a moment to round up the kids, I can drive you there," she offered.

"Thanks anyway, but that's not necessary.

I've got my other truck over at the office. It's only five blocks. I'll be fine."

He waved and she couldn't help returning his smile. He'd disappeared from view when she remembered that she'd wanted to tell him not to come around anymore. But she figured it was for the best. She owed him big-time. But that didn't mean they were going to be more than friends. No sirree. She wasn't about to let her mind dwell on romantic thoughts with this or any other firefighter.

Jared ate dinner at the restaurant later that night. It wasn't overly busy when he walked in. And he'd already scanned the room before he realized he was looking for Megan.

"Hi, Jared." Sean Nash sat with Tessa in a side booth and waved at him.

Another man sat across the table from them, with the same golden-brown hair and green eyes as Tessa. Ah, this must be her brother, Zach. Tim had mentioned the guy once. Apparently Zach was Sean's best friend.

Jared walked over to greet them all. "Hi, there."

"This is my brother, Zach," Tessa confirmed. "He's a member of the hotshot crew, too."

"Ah, I'm glad to meet you." Jared clasped

the hand that Zach extended, and they shook. Jared looked forward to meeting all the other hotshots. They were all seasonal employees, except for the superintendent and the crew boss, who were permanent hires employed twelve months out of the year. With the fire season just starting up, the crew members weren't all here yet.

Zach showed a genuine smile. "Likewise. I understand you're our new boss."

Jared nodded, then glanced at Sean. "Are you all ready for the rest of your team to return to work next week?"

"Yeah, it's been a long winter, but I'll get them back in shape real quick," Sean said. "We've got a couple of new hires. Some real good guys. They've worked on a few regular hand crews and passed our rigorous physical tests."

"Good. Has Brian approved them, too?"

"Yeah, he did. I'll get their hiring paperwork over to your office in the next couple of days."

"That'll be fine. It sounds like you've got everything under control," Jared said.

"Would you like to join us?" Tessa asked.

She was also a member of the hotshot crew. The only woman on the team. That was quite rare, but Jared had been told she could work most men under the table and she always carried her own weight.

He glanced around and noticed Caleb and June sitting in a far corner, chowing down on fried chicken and mashed potatoes and gravy. Jared had no doubt that Megan would be somewhere close by, and he had a strong urge to see her again. He tried to reason it away by telling himself that she was just one of his contractors and a friend. Nothing more.

"I don't want to intrude," he said.

"It's no intrusion." Zach scooted over to make room.

Jared felt a tap on his shoulder and turned.

Connie Wixler showed a wide smile. "Sorry, folks, but I'm afraid Jared is already spoken for tonight. Caleb is waiting for you over here. Come on."

Without waiting for his reply, the waitress headed toward the children's table. Jared smiled his apologies to Zach. "Sorry. I guess I'm having dinner with the kids tonight."

Zach's smile widened and he winked. "That's okay. Their mom's pretty special, too. Enjoy yourself."

Tessa and Sean flashed knowing grins. Jared ducked his head. He felt a moment of uncertainty but decided to ignore it. He wanted to explain that he and Megan were just friends, but he could see how some people might misconstrue their relationship. After all, they were both single and involved with each other—at least when it came to firefighting, to a certain degree.

Connie led him over to the booth. Caleb looked surprised to see him, but scrambled over to make a space for him. Jared couldn't help wondering if putting him at this table was all Connie's idea, and he figured the woman was still up to her old matchmaking tricks.

"Hi, Jared. Look what I got." The boy pulled a squiggly toy spider out of his pocket and dangled it in front of Jared's nose.

Jared laughed. "Yeah, that looks fun."

"I don't like it." June gave a shudder of disgust.

Caleb promptly thrust the spider at her, and she let out a little squeal. Several customers glanced their way.

"Now, stop that," Connie said.

"Yeah, you shouldn't tease your sister," Jared said.

That won a smile of approval from June. The boy showed a mischievous grin as Jared helped him stuff the spider back inside his pocket.

"What'll you have?" Connie asked, handing Jared a menu.

He handed it back and indicated the children's plates. "The same as the kids, with a tall glass of milk."

"Fried chicken and apple pie. It's the special tonight. Coming right up." Connie scurried away to put in his order.

"Are you gonna go out with our mom again?" Caleb asked as he took a drink of milk. When he pulled his glass away, he had a white mustache on his upper lip.

Jared smiled, helping the boy wipe his face with a napkin. "Actually, we weren't on a date before. We just happened to be at the same party over at Connie's house when your mom's truck broke down."

"But Sandy said it was a date."

"Sandy?" Jared said.

"Yeah, our babysitter. She said you were on a date with our mom. And June didn't like that," Caleb said.

Jared glanced at the little girl. She smacked her brother's shoulder with the palm of her hand. "I didn't say that, dummy."

"Yes, you did."

The girl ignored her brother and peered at Jared with suspicion. "Why do you want to go out with our mom?"

Wow! He never expected to get the second degree from these two children. Maybe he should have sat with the other hotshots, after all. But he kind of liked that these kids were looking out for their mother's best interests. It meant they were genuine. He also liked their open way of talking to him. It meant they trusted him enough to speak the truth. June seemed a bit withdrawn, but he'd won Caleb over hook, line and sinker. And he wondered why their approval mattered so much to him.

"I suppose it was sort of a blind date. But we didn't agree to it. We didn't know about it at the time. We were kind of set up by Connie and Tim," he hedged.

Caleb tilted his head to one side. "What do you mean a blind date? Can't you see our mom? She's right over there."

The boy pointed a finger to where Megan stood running the cash register. She looked up, saw her son pointing at her and flushed red as a new fire engine.

Jared glanced her way. She visibly flinched, then looked down as she counted out change for a customer. If Jared didn't know better, he'd think she was purposefully avoiding him tonight. And that was probably wise.

"That's not what he means." June bumped her brother's shoulder again. "He means he didn't ask Mom out and he didn't know they were gonna be on a date. Connie and Tim set it up without their permission."

"It wasn't a real date and I didn't…"

Jared trailed off. The kids were looking at him with open curiosity.

"I don't understand this blind-date stuff," Caleb said.

"It's when other people set you up with someone you don't know," June said.

"But you know our mommy," Caleb said.

Jared nodded. "Yes, that's right."

"So, how could your date with Mom be a blind date?"

"It's because we didn't agree to it," Jared said. "We didn't even know about it until after we arrived."

"Oh," Caleb said.

"But don't you like our mom?" June said, her voice vibrating with animosity.

Jared almost groaned. No matter what he said, there was no way to make them understand. He didn't want to cause a bigger problem by trying to explain.

"Of course I like her. I like her a lot," he said.

Caleb smiled and showed his sister a victorious grin. "See? I told you so."

June glared harder than ever.

A fissure of unease filtered through Jared's mind. Obviously the kids had discussed this issue among themselves in great detail. And he couldn't help wondering what else they'd said.

"You could ask Mom out again. We like you. Huh, June?" Caleb spoke with his mouth full of potatoes.

June stared at her plate, her forehead curved in a deep scowl. "You're not our dad."

"Of course I'm not," Jared agreed. "No one can ever take your father's place. I'd just like to be your mom's friend, if that's okay. I want to be your friend, too."

Friends was good. It was simple and uncomplicated. Jared held his breath, hoping that made the girl feel a tad better.

June's face softened and she looked up, her eyes meeting his. "Yes, I guess that's okay. But don't make mommy feel bad, okay? She's been real sad since our daddy died, and I don't want to see her cry anymore."

Jared's heart gave a powerful squeeze. Wow. He hadn't expected this but realized June was completely sincere. The thought of putting Megan into tears really tore at him. The little girl had driven home how serious this situation was. It was safer to let the subject drop.

He reached out and patted June's shoulder.

"Don't worry, sweetheart. I'd never do anything on purpose to hurt your mother. Or you kids, either."

June nodded and went back to eating. And that was that.

"So, how's the swing working out?" Jared asked, breathing a bit easier now that he'd passed the third degree.

"Great! I love it," Caleb gushed. Then his forehead crinkled in a troubled frown. "You should come over and try it out some time. But Mom would be there too, so you'd have to see her again. Is that okay?"

"Of course it's okay. I don't mind seeing your mother." Jared rubbed the boy's head.

Caleb smiled with delight. Jared realized the boy didn't understand the intricacies of dating, but he sure didn't want to explain it to him. No doubt it would get back to Megan, who might misunderstand and take it the wrong way.

"That might be nice." June smiled before scooping string beans into her mouth.

Jared almost groaned. His plan to remain neutral had officially backfired on him. Maybe he shouldn't have come here for supper tonight. Maybe he should have stayed home where it was lonely and safe and eaten a frozen dinner. Maybe…

He released a heavy sigh. His feelings had become so convoluted, even he was confused.

The situation only worsened when Connie delivered his meal. She set the plate of food in front of him with a grand flourish and a wide smile.

"Here you are. And can I just say, it's sure nice to see you and Megan getting so cozy?" the woman said.

Jared blinked, feeling as dazed and confused as Caleb had been earlier. "But I… We're not… We haven't…"

He couldn't finish. Anything he said might be misconstrued and taken out of context. After all, Megan was avoiding him like a plague of warts. She'd stayed far away from him since he'd walked into the restaurant. It could simply be that she was very busy tonight, yet he thought it was something more. Right now, he didn't know what to think. He tried to tell himself that he didn't want to get close to her, either, yet he'd come here for dinner and was now eating with her kids. How could he figure out what Megan wanted when he didn't know his own mind?

Just then he glanced up and saw her chatting with the group of hotshots. She worked as she talked, clearing a table next to them before wiping it down with a damp cloth.

Though he couldn't hear their words, he caught their laughter. Why did she seem to have such a negative attitude toward him when she was obviously friends with his crew members?

He bit into a juicy drumstick and noticed her surreptitious looks thrown his way. Or maybe he was just feeling self-conscious. He might be reading more into this situation than he should, and she was just keeping an eye on her children, to ensure they were doing okay. Her looks probably had nothing to do with him at all.

He finished his meal in record time. He said goodbye to the kids and stepped over to the cash register and pulled out his wallet. Not surprisingly, Megan was nowhere to be seen. She'd disappeared again.

"How was your dinner?" Connie asked as she stood before the cash register.

"Delicious. What do I owe you?" He looked up and waited.

"It's on the house." Connie leaned her hip against the counter and folded her arms.

He shook his head and pulled out some bills. "Nah, let me pay for my meal."

"No can do. The boss said it was part of your truck-rental agreement. Home-cooked meals for life."

"Not for life. No way." He shoved the bills at her, but she wouldn't take them.

Connie jerked her thumb toward the back office. "Besides, I'd get fired if I took your money."

Yeah, right. He wished Megan would forget about their truck agreement. But seeing the stubborn glint in Connie's eyes, he realized she would never relent.

He thrust his wallet back into his pocket. "Okay, tell Megan I said thank-you. The food was great tonight. I appreciate everything."

Connie gave him a knowing smile. "I'll tell her. And you stop by anytime." She leaned closer and whispered, "And do yourself a favor. Ask her out on a real date."

He stared. Surprised that she'd come right out and said what he knew she'd been thinking.

"Um, thanks," was his only response.

He turned and walked through the door to the parking lot. When he glanced over his shoulder, he saw through the wide windows that Megan had returned to the front of the restaurant. A low laugh escaped his throat. Yep, she had definitely been avoiding him. A good mother, who was probably thinking only about her kids. After all, he imagined a woman had to be careful what men she brought into the lives of her children.

Out of his peripheral vision, he saw that her gaze followed him as Connie stood chatting beside her. No doubt the waitress was telling Megan everything he'd said.

He got into his truck. And he drove home, feeling lonelier than ever before.

Chapter Six

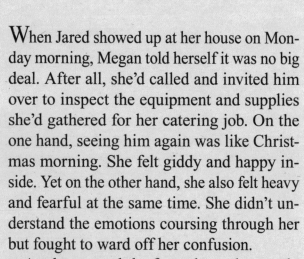

When Jared showed up at her house on Monday morning, Megan told herself it was no big deal. After all, she'd called and invited him over to inspect the equipment and supplies she'd gathered for her catering job. On the one hand, seeing him again was like Christmas morning. She felt giddy and happy inside. Yet on the other hand, she also felt heavy and fearful at the same time. She didn't understand the emotions coursing through her but fought to ward off her confusion.

As she opened the front door, she caught the scent of rain. A lightning storm in the night had washed her green lawn, making it glimmer in the morning sunlight. Stepping back, she admitted Jared to her living room.

"Hi, there. I brought your truck over from

the repair shop. They finally have it ready." Jared showed that endearing smile.

"You picked up my truck from the garage?"

"Yeah, I hope you don't mind. I thought it'd save you some bother if you didn't have to drag the kids all the way there and back."

She glanced past his shoulder, looking outside. Sure enough, her rusty old truck sat parked in her driveway. Grant must have finally gotten the parts in and finished his work.

"It's running great," Jared said, "but I'd still rather you use the one I lent you when you drive up on the mountain. It's newer and I think it's more reliable."

She shook her head. "You didn't need to bring my truck over. I'd already settled the bill with Grant yesterday, but I didn't plan to pick it up until later this afternoon."

"It's no bother."

"Well, thanks for saving me the trouble. Grant has had it over two weeks and I was beginning to give up hope of ever seeing it again. It ended up needing a complete engine rebuild."

"Yeah, car failures are the pits. And expensive, too. I'm sorry it broke down." Jared handed her the key while she closed the front door.

His gaze clouded over, and he looked away and she realized the guards were up between them. An invisible wall she didn't know how to breach even if she wanted to try. Which she didn't.

"I appreciate you coming over. My equipment is in the garage." She led the way through the kitchen, conscious of him trailing behind her.

"Where are the kids today?" He followed her out into the backyard.

She glanced at the swing hanging from the tall tree and remembered the day he'd hooked it up for her children. They'd enjoyed it nonstop ever since. "They're over at a friend's house, having a playdate. They'll be home in an hour. I thought it would make our meeting easier if we didn't have them interrupting us every five seconds."

Jared chuckled. "I don't mind. I've become pretty good friends with Caleb and June."

Yes, she'd noticed. Although June was still a bit reluctant, she was slowly warming up to the man. And Caleb adored him. Megan liked him, too. A lot. And if she let down her guard, it'd be so easy to fall madly, deeply…

No! She couldn't think that way.

"Last Thursday was their last day of school. I'm trying to find ways to keep them busy during the summer break while spending some quality time with them, too. Tonight, we're going to watch a movie and eat popcorn together."

He slid one hand into his pants pocket. "That sounds fun. I imagine being a single working mom poses a lot of challenges. But you seem to handle it all with a smile."

"Thank you. From what I've seen, you're good with kids, too."

Oh, stupid. She shouldn't have said that.

"Well, it's easy when they're as sweet as Caleb and June. They've got a good mom," he said.

Ah, that melted her heart as nothing else could.

"Thank you. Why haven't you ever married?" The moment Megan asked the question, she regretted it. It was too bold. Too personal. But she really wanted to know.

His eyes widened in surprise. "Actually, I was married once."

Now it was her turn to be startled. "Really?"

"Yeah, but it didn't work out. Sharon hated the small, remote towns I dragged her to live in for my profession. She was a city girl through and through. While I was working up in the mountains, she found someone else she wanted more than me."

Oh, boy. Megan wasn't prepared for that much information. She didn't know what to say. What to think. And she honestly couldn't imagine why any woman would ever toss this handsome man over for someone else.

"I'm so sorry, Jared. I didn't mean to pry," she said.

He gave a low laugh, but there was no humor in it. "It's okay. Actually, it feels kind of good to finally talk about it. You're the first person I've mentioned it to since it happened."

She heard the hurt in his voice and felt like a heel for reminding him of his painful history. She didn't want to be the person he confided in. It brought them closer somehow, and she couldn't allow that. No, not at all.

He took a deep breath, as though he were gathering his courage. "It's in the past and I need to move on now."

She was trying to do the same with her own life, and she realized how much they had in common. Both of them had been hurt deeply. Both of them had former loves they were still trying to get past. And honestly, she didn't think she could ever get over losing Blaine.

They stepped beyond the backyard. It widened up into a spacious lot, partitioned by a lawn area with a swing set, a small garden and a tall fence. The mobile kitchen and a semitruck sat off to one side. And Megan resolved to focus on business again.

"I've made a number of contacts," she said, "to hire several more cooks and some high school kids to help cater the meals to the fire crews. If we get a fire in our mountains, I'll be ready."

"That's good."

Opening the door to the garage, she flipped on the light. She blinked, letting her eyes become accustomed to the dim interior. Jared did likewise, gazing at the shelves filled with tools and camping and yard equipment.

She pointed at several rolls of colored tape sitting on the workbench. "I'm planning to color code the boxes of food, to ensure things like pancakes don't get sent out to the spike camps without butter and syrup to accompany them."

He nodded and gave a low sound of approval. "Great! I can't tell you how many times I've had to eat a dry loaf of bread and apples with nothing but water to wash them down because the caterer didn't send us any meat and cheese to go with it. Just bread and apples."

She made a little grimace. "That wouldn't be much of a meal for a hungry firefighter."

"Yeah, it isn't. But when you're out there working like a dog, you'll eat anything you can get."

That made her laugh. She liked this man's sense of humor and hard-work ethic. Not to mention his gorgeous smile. He was close to perfect. But they wouldn't even be having this conversation if he wasn't a hotshot. If she ever gave another man a chance, he'd have a job she was sure would bring him home every night.

Once more, she resolved to keep her distance.

"Um, will you still need some Cubitainers for things like milk, juice and water?" Jared asked, trying to focus his thoughts back on work. Megan's question about his marriage had left him feeling a bit uneasy. And yet, it felt good to finally talk about his divorce. He'd kept it all bottled up inside of him for so long that it actually relieved some tension to speak the words out loud.

She nodded. "Yes, if you can get them for me."

"Do you have the necessary dining tables and chairs for people to sit on?"

Her long ponytail bounced as she nodded her head. "Yes. And the kitchen trailer includes deep fryers, grills and even a tilt skillet for preparing scrambled eggs and mashed potatoes."

"That sounds great," he said.

"I've also got some additional insulated containers, warming ovens, a propane refrigerator chest and a trailer to haul it all up onto the mountain." She pointed at each item stacked neatly beside the trailer and a sturdy tarp to cover everything with, in case it rained.

He liked the note of confidence in her voice. The expression of buoyancy on her face. She'd been working hard, and he realized he'd made the right call by giving her the contract.

She stepped past him to display the rows of canned foods she'd already purchased from her grocery supplier and set aside for when she needed it.

Her arm brushed against his chest, and he sucked back a quick inhale. After his divorce, he thought he was immune to ever being attracted to another woman. But that had changed with Megan.

"I can get the Cubitainers in for you next week," he said, wishing he could keep his mind on their task.

"That should be soon enough. Any idea when we'll get our first fire in the area?"

"No telling. The weather's been dry and warm, which provides a lot of tinder for the lightning storms we've been having."

He paused, taking a deep inhale. Even in the musty garage, he caught her clean, fragrant scent.

Time to go.

"I'll bring the Cubitainers over as soon as they come in," he said.

"That will be fine."

She walked with him out to the front of the house.

"Thanks for coming over," she said.

He smiled, liking the way the sun highlighted streaks of gold in her hair. "Anytime."

As he climbed into his truck, he felt light and cheerful inside, and he didn't know why. He'd confided some personal things to Megan, yet he knew without asking that she understood how he was feeling. And that she'd keep his confidence.

Having her to lean on was not something he

could get used to, though. Because he wasn't ready for another relationship—even with someone as capable and pretty as Megan.

Chapter Seven

A persistent ringing woke Megan. Cracking her eyes open just a bit, she squinted into the darkness. A quick glance at the bedside clock told her it was just after three in the morning.

Ring!

She reached for the phone, knocking the clock off the bedside table in the process. It clattered to the floor. Who on earth could be calling her at this time of the night?

"Hello?" she answered, her voice sounding groggy.

"Good morning! You awake yet?"

Jared's words made her eyes pop open wide. At first, she was confused. But then, her senses returned.

She chuckled. "I am now."

"Sorry to disturb you so early, but we've got a fire. It isn't big, yet. Just fifteen hundred acres, but it's zero contained," he said, his voice upbeat but also serious.

Megan rubbed her eyes, which were gritty with fatigue. She'd received these calls in the past. So had Blaine. They'd come from a different FMO back then, but he'd always sounded energetic and ready to face the coming fire.

"How many workers will we need to feed today?" she asked.

"Two hundred men and women have been called in this morning, with about fifty administrative people to run the incident command post. They've called in several more hotshot crews, which will be arriving later this afternoon. You should plan to feed about four hundred people for dinner tonight."

Whew! Good thing she had enough T-bone steaks stashed in the freezer chest. "Okay, I can handle it."

"I'll be up on the mountain by the time you reach the fire camp." He then proceeded to give her instructions on how to get there.

"Do you know the area?" he asked.

"Yes, I've been there before."

"Good. Just drive carefully and stay safe," he said.

His caring words sent a tingle of warmth up her spine. "I will. And you, too."

As she hung up the phone, she realized what she'd said. They sounded like a pair of good friends looking out for each other. And they weren't friends. Not really. And yet, she couldn't help worrying about him, and the other hotshots, too.

Shaking her head, she hurried to make some phone calls of her own. Her team was on standby and knew she might call them at any time, day or night.

By nine o'clock that morning, she'd notified her crew, loaded up the trailer, buckled her kids into their seats and was driving her truck along the winding mountain road. They hit a bump that jarred them all, and June gasped. As Megan watched closely for some sign of the wildfire base camp, she was grateful Jared had insisted she use his more reliable truck.

Her crew drove in tandem. She led the way, followed by Frank driving the semi with the mobile kitchen attached. Catherine Brindley, a school lunch cook, and four high school seniors with enough maturity to help with this job, were in a van bringing up the rear. They'd be staying up on the mountain for several days, until Megan brought in another crew to relieve them of their work. She'd hired a couple more cooks and waitresses to man the diner in town, but Megan wanted Frank's expertise to help set up their operations at the fire camp.

The trailer hitched to Megan's truck thumped behind at an even clip. It was filled with cooler chests, canned vegetables, fresh salad mix and bags of potatoes for baking. She had enough bacon, eggs, pancake mix, meat, bread, potato chips, trail mix and fruit to make breakfast and lunch for tomorrow. By then, she'd be back up here with another load of food. While the fire lasted, she figured this would be a daily trip, shuttling between the restaurant in town and the fire camp in the mountains. No doubt it'd take a toll on her, but she wanted to ensure everything ran smoothly. And she'd be paid well for her labors, the money a welcome blessing.

Just off the smooth asphalt, she saw a red sign with a black arrow pointing to the west that said Incident Base Camp. This must be it. An alpine meadow high in the Sierra Nevada Mountains. The large clearing was filled with red Indian paintbrush, now trampled beneath hundreds of boot heels and tires from large, heavy equipment. Bulldozers, pumper trucks and water tenders. You name it. They were all here, lined up in tidy rows and ready for action.

Clusters of men wearing a variety of yellow Nomex fireproof shirts, windbreakers, spruce-green pants and heavy Vibram-soled boots were moving around the camp in a melee of organized chaos. To the north, the office district had been set up where the operations of the camp took place. Long mobile offices with the words *Finance* and *Check-in* stood off to the side near the entrance. Moving nice and slow, Megan pulled into the camp, wondering where Jared wanted them to set up.

"This is it," she said to her kids.

Caleb and June sat beside her, their eyes wide as they craned their necks to see everything.

Megan gazed toward the south, where dozens of little tents dotted the landscape. Undoubtedly, this was the residential area, where hundreds of men and women slept, ate and got their orders before going out on the fire line each day. A miniature city. From the looks of things, Megan's catering crew would be up here serving meals for a couple of weeks. Maybe more.

She parked the truck near the check-in. "Stay here. I'll be right back."

Sitting in a booster seat beside his sister, Caleb snapped off his seat belt and leaned against the dashboard. "But I wanna go with you, Mom. I wanna see Jared."

Megan inwardly groaned. Maybe she shouldn't have brought her kids with her. But she wanted to spend more time with them. She'd brought them along, thinking they wouldn't be here long.

"Remember we talked about this? We're just dropping off supplies, setting up the kitchen, and then we're going back down the mountain into town. I don't want you to get into any trouble," she said.

"I just want to see Jared," Caleb grumbled.

"He's working. You know that, son."

"Where is Jared?" June asked as she gazed out the windshield.

Megan opened her door. "I'm sure he's here somewhere. I'll be right back."

She got out and went to tell Catherine and Frank what she was doing. No sense in everyone getting out of their vehicles right now if they were in the wrong place.

As she approached, Frank rolled down the window of the semi and rested his beefy arm against the outside of the door.

"I'm going to find out where we should set up. Would you mind keeping an eye on the kids for a few minutes?" She pointed to where the kids still remained safely inside her truck, craning their heads this way and that as they looked out the windows.

He waved a hand. "Sure will. I'll wait right here until you tell me where I should go."

It wasn't long before Megan had checked in and received instructions on where to unload their food supplies. As she returned to her truck, she caught herself staring at each man she passed. Some wore yellow or red hard hats, others wore baseball caps, and it dawned on her that she too was looking for Jared. She couldn't help wondering why that was. She was a mature woman and knew what she was doing. So why was she eager to see him again?

Back in the truck, she turned on the vehicle and drove toward the east side of the command center. The semi groaned as Frank put it in gear and followed behind, with Catherine and the high school kids in pursuit. They all parked near a wide, empty area on the west side of the camp, then hopped out and gathered around for instructions.

"Let's put up the tent right here with the kitchen over there. I think that will give us the best advantage of sunlight throughout the day." Megan pointed to indicate where everything should go.

The crew went to work, opening up the trailer and unloading boxes.

"There's Jared!" Caleb pointed and would have run toward the man, but Megan latched onto his arm.

"Stay here. He'll come to us." She didn't want her boy running around the fire camp. Not with all the big, noisy equipment moving around.

Sure enough, Jared came striding toward them, wearing a white hard hat, his Forest Service shirt, spruce-green pants and heavy fire boots. He looked handsome, strong and in control, and Megan's heart gave a powerful thump.

"Let me go, Mom. I want to see him." Caleb strained against her hand, and his eagerness surprised her.

"You've got to wait," June said. Being the big sister, she tugged on Caleb's shoulders.

"We're going to see him, but you kids stay with me. Remember what I told you about safety while we're up here? No wandering off, or I won't be able to bring you up here again," Megan told her children.

"Okay," Caleb grouched.

Both kids nodded obediently, but that flew right out the window the moment Megan let go of Caleb's hand. He raced toward the firefighter, screaming with joy.

"Jared! Jared!"

"Hi, Caleb." Jared welcomed the boy with a big smile and open arms.

Caleb hugged him tight. As Jared swung him around, the child's laughter filled the air. June stayed beside her mother, seeming a bit ambivalent toward the FMO. Megan felt a hard lump of ice form in the pit of her stomach. Her son loved this man. Which made it even more difficult to pull away from him. And once more, she regretted bringing her kids up on the mountain with her today.

"Hi, there." Carrying Caleb, Jared greeted Megan with a smile that sucked the air right out of her lungs.

"Hello." She forced herself to look away as she set a box of canned corn on top of the growing pile.

"Let me call a camp crew over to help. We'll have you set up in no time," Jared said.

He set Caleb on his feet, then sauntered off and returned moments later with five strapping young men wearing blue jeans, long-sleeved shirts and work boots. They didn't hesitate before they each pulled on their leather gloves and went to work. Megan was startled at how quickly they got everything unloaded.

Next, they started laying out the tent. With people stationed on all four sides, they spread the heavy canvas across the ground, pulling and stretching until it was a wide oblong shape. The barracks-style tent was huge, large enough to cover tables and chairs to seat three hundred people at one time. After arranging the support lines, they installed the wooden masts to hold the tent up.

"Pull!" Megan called to the men.

In unison, they lifted the masts and the tent rose slowly into the air. Caleb stood near her, pressing his tongue against his upper lip as he grunted and helped Tim Wixler tug on the line with all his might. As the tent rose into the air, June giggled and hurried beneath it, staring straight up at the heavy canvas. She stood near Jared, who was installing the center mast.

Crack!

The sound of a gunshot caused Megan to jerk her head around. June looked at her mom, her eyes wide with alarm. Megan couldn't tell where the sound had come from.

"Look out!" one of the men yelled.

Another crack sounded, like the snap of a heavy timber. Megan stared in confusion.

A sick feeling settled in her stomach. Something was wrong, but she didn't know what.

At that moment, Jared darted in front of June, placing his own body protectively at the fore. Simultaneously, the center mast broke in two, the top portion hurtling through the air toward Jared. It struck him solidly across the chest with a sickening thud. He grunted and reared his head back, as though the air had been knocked out of his body. Blood spattered into the air, and he jerked his hand up to his chin. Red oozed from between his fingers. The broken mast must have clipped his chin, slicing though his flesh.

"Jared!" Megan cried.

He was injured! And in a fraction of time, Megan knew that without him there, the heavy mast would have struck June across the head.

The tent quivered and swayed. The tension on the support lines was too much. Like a slingshot, they whipped free of their bindings, and the tent started to collapse in on itself. The workers scrambled to get out of the way.

"June!" Megan raced toward her daughter, but too late. Jared and the little girl disappeared beneath the voluminous folds of the heavy tent.

A lance of fear speared Megan's chest. Just

one thought pounded her brain. June! She had to get her daughter to safety. And Jared. He was obviously wounded. But just how serious the injury was, she didn't have a clue.

Megan thrust Caleb toward the cook. "Stay here with Frank."

Frank took hold of Caleb's arm to keep him there. Satisfied that her son was safe, Megan turned and ran toward her daughter. Without the support of the rest of the tent, another mast fell directly in front of her. It barely missed her as she lurched back in surprise.

People were yelling, running to help. The tent hit the ground, causing puffs of dirt to rise up in its wake. Megan watched in helpless horror, circling the perimeter of the canvas, searching for a way inside. A large bump and ripple of movement beneath the canvas told her exactly where Jared and June were located beneath the heavy tarp. Megan couldn't see her daughter, but she could hear her frantic screams. Over and over, June yelled. And every instinct inside of Megan was desperate to reach her daughter.

"Mommy! Help!" the child sobbed.

"I'm coming," Megan called back.

And then, Jared emerged from beneath the tarp. He clawed his way out with one hand while he carried June in his other arm. The moment they broke free of the tent, the girl stopped screaming, but tears ran down her face and she cried hysterically.

"Mommy! Oh, Mommy." The child sniffled and reached for her mother.

Megan enfolded June into her arms, hushing her tears. She searched to ensure the girl was all right, with no bones broken. "Are you hurt?"

June shook her head, still wailing with fear. The child was visibly shaken by the mishap but appeared to be all right.

"There, sweetheart. I'm here. Are you okay now?" Megan asked.

June nodded, wiping her eyes with her hands. "Uh-huh. I'm okay. Jared. He...he saved me."

The girl cast a look of teary disbelief toward the man.

Megan looked up, stunned by this event. Jared stood looking at her, a gash on his chin dripping blood. He swayed on his feet, and she wondered if he had a head injury.

"Jared, you're hurt." Megan clasped his arm, trying to steady him.

"I'll be fine." But he staggered, going down on one knee, pulling her with him. His chin dropped to his chest, his eyes vacant. For a moment, Megan thought he might pass out. He obviously wasn't all right.

"Come on, men. Take his arms." Tim waved at a couple of the workers, and they took hold of Jared, lifting him up. "Quick! Let's get him over to the first-aid station."

Without discussion, they headed across the camp toward the medic unit. Watching them go, Megan longed to follow. To make sure Jared was okay. But she knew she needed to stay here with her children. The first-aid trailer wasn't overly large, and the last thing they needed was extra people clogging it up. But she couldn't help fretting. Jared could be badly injured. And she realized that, if the broken mast could bring this tall, strong man to his knees, then what might it have done to June? Megan had no doubt that Jared's quick thinking had saved her little daughter's life.

"Mommy, Jared saved me," June said again, her chin quivering.

"Yes, sweetheart. He did." Megan hugged the girl tight. Together, they watched the men carry Jared up the steps to the first-aid trailer, and they disappeared inside.

Caleb tugged on Megan's shirttail. "Is Jared gonna be all right, Mom?"

"Of course he is," Frank said, ruffling the boy's hair.

But Megan wasn't so sure. She was worried about him, too, and she didn't like that emotion. She'd vowed never to fret over another firefighter. Because worrying meant she cared, which was the one thing she'd promised she wouldn't do ever again. And yet, she couldn't seem to help it. And that scared her most of all.

Two days later, Jared stepped around the side of the mobile kitchen and headed toward the supply tent. Holding an arm across his abdomen, he walked slowly, conscious of his bruised ribs. He was moving a bit better since he'd been pummeled by the broken tent mast, but he was still mighty sore. One of the men had told him that Megan had just arrived in the fire camp with a load of fresh supplies, and he wanted to ensure that she and the kids were okay.

The acrid scent of fire filtered over the air. Drifts of gray smoke filled the afternoon sky, making the sun look like a red fireball. The fire had expanded to three thousand acres, but was now 30 percent contained.

Men were lined up in front of the mobile kitchen, moving through the chow line in steady rhythm. Their laughter and carefree banter told him they were happy.

"Step right up and get it. I've got mashed or baked potatoes today. Which will you have?" Frank's booming voice called to the next man up.

Jared walked over to the canopy, where the food supplies were being stored. As he passed, he listened to the men's comments.

"They've sure improved the food on this fire," one of them said.

"Yeah, the steaks are tender and juicy. And I'm gonna have myself a thick slice of chocolate cake right after," another man said.

Jared smiled. It was clear that Megan and her people were doing a great job. And he wasn't surprised.

Lifting his head, he saw her step up into the back of her carry trailer. Wearing leather gloves, she emerged moments later with a large box of canned beans. He could tell the contents from the stamp on the outside of the cardboard, and her tense expression told him the weight must be heavy. Her bare arms looked too slender to carry such a load. Without waiting for permission, he stepped over and lifted the box out of her hands.

"Jared!" She jerked back and looked up, her eyes widening in surprise.

He smiled and set the box on top of the others in the back of the mobile kitchen.

"Hi, there. You don't need to do this heavy work. I can get a camp crew over here to unload all of this for you."

Before she could reply, he called and waved his arms to get the attention of three young men standing nearby. They jogged over to them and, with a few short instructions, Jared told them what to do. They immediately set to work and had the trailer unloaded in record time.

"You're going to spoil me," Megan said.

"It's just part of the job," Jared said.

She nodded and gazed at the tidy stacks of bottled water, Gatorade and boxes of buns and frozen hamburger patties. What had taken the camp workers only a matter of minutes to complete would have taken her an hour or more of work.

"Thank you," she said, smiling at each man in turn. She handed each one of them a bag of roasted almonds and a candy bar.

They grinned with delight and accepted her gift before returning to their other chores. Finally, Megan turned to face Jared.

"Where are the kids today?" he asked.

She lifted a hand. "I left them in town with a child care provider. I...I thought it was safer."

He frowned. "I hope the tent mishap didn't scare them off. I think that was just a fluke."

She shrugged. "Maybe I'll bring them up again sometime. But not right now."

He noticed her gaze centering on his face where he had eight stitches and a small bandage covering his chin.

"How are you feeling?" she asked.

"Except for some sore ribs, I'm good."

She stepped near and handed him a package of salted nuts. "Are you sure you ought to be back to work so soon? When I tried to check on you yesterday, they said they'd taken you to the hospital in Reno by Care Flight so you could have some X-rays. Then Connie told me that Tim said you might have a concussion. I called the hospital, but they wouldn't tell me anything about your condition."

He shrugged off her concern. "No, not a concussion. The broken mast clipped my chin, but it struck my rib cage. Really, I'm fine. Just a few bruises and this."

He gestured to his chin, wishing his injury wasn't so obvious. He'd be glad when it healed enough to remove the ugly bandage. No doubt he'd have a small scar there to remind him of what had happened. But it was a small price to pay to keep June safe.

Megan lifted a hand toward his face, her eyes creased with sympathy. Her fingertips brushed against his cheek, and he felt her touch like the flutter of butterfly wings against his skin. Then she lowered her hand and took a deep breath, as though she were steadying her nerves. "I'm sorry you got hurt. But I'm beyond grateful for what you did. If you hadn't interceded, that mast would have struck June. I hate to think what might have happened to my little girl."

He agreed with Megan's last comment. June could have been seriously injured or worse. But her gratitude and the fact that she'd gone to such lengths to find out if he was okay touched him deeply.

"June is okay, then?" he asked.

"Yes, she's fine. Thanks to you."

Her words made him a bit uncomfortable. At the time, he'd acted without thinking about his own safety. He only knew that he'd given Megan his word that he'd keep her and her people safe while they worked at the fire camp. And in that split instant when he'd realized June was in danger, he was determined to protect her no matter what.

"I'm just glad I could help. But it wasn't any big deal," he said.

"I disagree," she said. "You saved my

daughter's life, yet you were hurt in the process. And I'm so grateful, Jared. Thank you for what you did."

He smiled, her gratitude a refreshing change. His ex-wife had seemed to do nothing but criticize him. With her, he couldn't do anything right. It felt good to be appreciated for once. "It was my pleasure."

And he meant it.

"It just reinforces in my mind how dangerous a fire camp can be. I never should have brought the kids up here with me that day. I thought it'd be a simple trip, but we had too much work to do with putting up the tent and all," she said.

"It was a rare situation," he said. "I hope you'll bring them up again when you're just delivering supplies."

She looked doubtful, and he decided not to push the issue.

"Well, I better get on my way. I've got to get back to the restaurant." She pulled off her gloves, tucked them into her pants pocket, then wiped her hands nervously against her blue jeans.

"Yeah, I wouldn't want you on the mountain roads in the dark. Give the kids my best," he said.

"I will." She walked around to the side of her truck and climbed into the driver's seat.

Within moments, she'd started up the engine and pulled away. Watching her go, Jared struggled with his tangled emotions. In spite of his best efforts not to, he felt protective toward Megan and her two children. But his feelings seemed to go deeper than that, and he was irritated and confused by his attraction toward the pretty widow.

A sound behind him caused Jared to turn. Tim Wixler stood nearby, reaching into the watering trough for a bottle of chilled water. Watching Megan drive away, the man popped the lid and took a long swallow before he smiled.

"You're spending a bit more time around the mess hall than usual, aren't you?" Tim said.

Jared shrugged. "So?"

Tim's gaze followed Megan's truck as it rumbled down the dirt road. Her brake lights flashed as she turned onto the main road. "So, I can't say as I blame you. She's pretty and a mighty fine gal."

Jared didn't pretend not to catch Tim's meaning. He wasn't the only one that had noticed the electricity humming between him and Megan. Other people were bound to notice it, too. But Jared couldn't have any special interest in Megan other than her work. No matter what, he had to keep it all about business and nothing more.

"She's just one of our new vendors—that's all. I want to make sure she has what she needs. And I wanted to ask if June was all right," Jared said.

Tim nodded, a wide grin curving his thick lips. A chuckle erupted from his wide chest. "Yeah, sure. I understand perfectly."

The man sauntered away, and Jared stared after him. But he didn't say another word. He kept telling himself that he had no interest whatsoever in the pretty caterer. Their relationship was purely professional. That was all. But deep in his heart, he knew he felt something more. Something he didn't understand and feared more than he dared to admit. He was attracted to Megan Rocklin. He liked her and her two sweet little kids. And because of what he'd gone through with his ex-wife, those kinds of feelings filled him with more than a little bit of fear.

Chapter Eight

"Hey, there. You busy?"

Jared looked up and saw Sean Nash standing in the doorway to his Forest Service office. Sean leaned against the doorjamb and slipped his thumbs through his belt loops.

Jared set his ballpoint on top of the wildfire contracts he'd been preparing and glanced at the wall clock. Four thirty-eight in the afternoon. He'd been so engrossed in his work that he'd lost track of time. The wildfire was out, and he'd returned to town late last night. Now, he was playing catch-up on his office work.

"Hi. Not too busy. What's up?" Jared's chair squeaked as he sat back.

"I just brought in those incident reports you requested. I gave them to Hannah at the front desk."

"Good. Thanks for bringing them in so quickly," Jared said.

"No problem." Sean turned to leave but hesitated. "Hey, are you planning to go to the forest supervisor's retirement party?"

Jared lifted his arms high above his head and stretched, barely feeling the movement in his sore rib cage. "Of course I'm planning to go."

Politically, he couldn't miss it. The forest supervisor was the big boss over the entire Minoa National Forest. His retirement party was a big deal. It'd be held in Reno, in the ballroom of the convention center. Most of the employees working on this national forest were expected to attend. Including him.

Sean grinned. "Are you bringing a date?"

Jared jerked his arms down, wrenching a shoulder muscle in the process. He grimaced, not liking where this topic was headed.

"Um, I doubt it," he said.

"Tessa and I could fix you up with someone," Sean said.

A blaze of terror washed over Jared, and he held up a hand. "No, thanks. No more blind dates."

"What about Megan?"

Jared shook his head. "What do you mean?"

"Are you interested in her?"

Wow, that was blunt. But it made Jared stop and stare. Was he interested in the pretty widow? He didn't want to be, but he still felt the undeniable attraction between them.

"Why do you ask?" Jared hedged.

Sean tilted his head in a warning frown. "I overheard Harlie say that if you don't ask her out, he's planning to invite her to go to the retirement party with him. I just thought you should know."

Jared's throat tightened. He tried not to care who was interested in Megan, but a blaze of jealousy burned through his veins. He didn't want her going out with any man. Not unless it was him. And that wasn't fair, to either of them. If he didn't want anything to do with her, then it shouldn't matter who she dated. Should it?

"Why don't you ask Megan to go with you?" Sean suggested.

Megan. Yes, she was safe enough. Jared enjoyed being with her. But he didn't want to ask her out on a date. Working with her as a caterer was one thing, but going out with her was another. He still wasn't ready for that. Maybe he never would be.

"If not Megan, Tessa and I could set you up with another gal we know. She lives over in Gardnerville. A real nice lady. Just a few years older than you. An attorney. She's never been married and doesn't have any kids. No entanglements to bog you down."

"I kind of like kids," Jared said, thinking of Megan and her two children.

Sean arched his brows. "Is that so?"

"Yes, but no thanks."

"Well, I've got a warning for you. If you don't have someone lined up, the guys are talking about setting you up on another blind date."

The guys. That meant the hotshot crew. And Jared didn't dare consider what they might do and who they might fix him up with without his knowledge. He knew how tenacious they could be. If he wasn't careful, he could find himself out with a less-than-desirable partner and have a miserable evening. He had to do something fast to stop it.

"Tell the guys I'll have someone with me, so they shouldn't do something crazy."

Sean chuckled. "Smart guy. All right, I'll tell them. But you know, Megan has been to these things before, when her husband was alive. She knows the lay of the land and how to navigate these types of parties. You want me to ask her for you?"

Horror ignited inside of Jared's mind. The last thing he wanted was for Sean to ask

Megan on a date for him. This wasn't high school, after all. So why did he feel like an awkward teenager? But if Jared didn't bring a date, he wouldn't get off so easily the next time. He knew how it worked. The members of the hotshot crew would never let him live it down. They'd be setting him up left and right, no matter what he said.

"Of course not. I'm set," Jared insisted.

"So, who are you bringing then?"

"You'll have to wait and see. But rest assured that I've got plans."

Or at least, he would have before this day was through. No way was he going on another blind date. The thought made his stomach churn. His instincts told him that he couldn't do better than Megan. In fact, he couldn't seem to get her off his mind, no matter how hard he tried. But he'd never hear the end of it if he didn't show up to the retirement party with a date.

Maybe he *should* invite Megan to go with him to the retirement party. They'd had fun at the barbecue, playing charades. She was laid-back and easy to talk to. She smiled readily. And when he walked into the retirement party with her on his arm, he could avoid any unwelcome entanglements. Of course, it could backfire on him, too. Everyone would think he and Megan were an item. But he could simply explain that they were just friends. Friends was good, wasn't it?

"Do you and your date want to ride into Reno with Tessa and me?" Sean asked, rubbing his bristly chin.

"Nah. I'll take my own vehicle. But thanks for the offer." Jared tried to sound casual.

He tried to play it cool but wondered how to ask Megan. After all, she wasn't interested in dating, either, if he was reading her vibes correctly.

And what if she said no? Then, who would he invite? He couldn't show up to the party alone. Not if he hoped to never be faced with another blind date he hadn't counted on.

Sean smiled and braced himself off the doorjamb. "Well, I better get going. Talk to you later."

The man turned and walked out, and Jared breathed a sigh of relief. He knew by this time tomorrow, Sean would have told everyone in the office and on the hotshot crew that he had a date for the party. And everyone would be speculating who that was. And right then, Jared wished he wasn't an only child. If only he had a sister or other family member, he'd call and beg them to accompany him. But he didn't have a sister, or a mom or even a cousin. In fact, the only woman friend he could think of was Megan.

Jared shook his head. He'd put this off long enough. The party was less than two weeks away. If he didn't want to have egg on his face and make the matter even worse, he'd better come up with someone to accompany him. And fast.

Megan stood in the back of the restaurant, filling the industrial-strength dishwasher with drinking glasses. She added the detergent, closed the door, flipped the locking lever and pressed the start button. A low whoosh of water filled the air as the machine started its wash cycle.

Stepping back, she leaned against the counter for several moments, catching her breath. The wildfire was out, and her catering crew had returned to town late last night, exhausted and filthy. Megan had spent most of the day cleaning the mobile kitchen and all of the equipment. With Catherine's help, she'd restocked their supplies. It'd been a big job, but they needed to be ready at a moment's notice, in case they got called out on another fire.

Picking up a rack of clean coffee cups and saucers, she headed out into the restaurant to put them away. Cindy, one of the new waitresses she'd been training over the past week, stood leaning against the front counter. She lifted a hand, laughing in a carefree manner.

Megan rounded the corner and caught sight of who Cindy was talking to.

Jared!

The moment she saw the handsome fire management officer, Megan's senses went on high alert. She hadn't expected to see him again so soon, but it wouldn't have mattered if she did. Every time he walked into the room, it was the same. She felt all mushy inside, and her knees became weak and wobbly.

He sat on one of the bar stools and leaned his elbows on the front counter while Cindy took his order. At nineteen years of age, the girl was a bit young for Jared. But that didn't stop her from giggling at something funny he'd said.

Megan cleared her throat loudly. Simultaneously, Cindy and Jared whirled toward her. In a rather furtive gesture, Cindy ducked her head. Megan had made a point of telling the girl to be polite but not overly chatty with their customers. Cindy had work to do and needed to focus on her chores. Since they knew most of their diners, it was easy to spend too much time visiting.

"Okay, I've got it." Cindy jotted a few more notes on her pad of paper before turning to snap Jared's order up for Martha, their new morning cook.

The waitress scurried over to take the orders of two men who had just walked in and sat waiting in a booth.

"Hi there." Megan sauntered over to the counter, where she began stacking the cups near the coffeepot.

"Hi, Megan," Jared said.

"She's a bit young for you, don't you think?" She glanced over her shoulder, trying to keep her voice light and teasing, but she feared she sounded rather jealous instead.

Jared lifted one brow. "Who? Cindy?"

Megan just laughed, trying to ignore the green jealousy coursing through her veins. After all, it wasn't her business who Jared was interested in. She certainly didn't care. Right?

"Yeah, she's way too young for me," he agreed with a chuckle. "I'm just friends with her dad. He's a local rancher we recently contracted for the use of his bulldozer when we have a wildfire in the area."

So Jared wasn't interested in Cindy. He was just being nice because of who the girl's father was. Though she fought it, Megan was pleased enormously by that news.

She turned and wiped down the already-clean countertops. "What are you having today?"

"My usual."

"Would you like a glass of orange juice?" she asked.

"Yes, please."

Again with the nice manners.

"I'll get it," she said.

He reached out and touched her hand. She jerked and went very still, meeting his eyes.

"Actually, before you do that, I was hoping to ask you something," he said.

She drew back and waited, her fingers choking the damp cloth. Every time this man asked her something, she ended up agreeing to things she didn't want. She just couldn't seem to tell him no.

"Okay, shoot," she said, trying to be brave.

"In a couple of weeks, there's a special Forest Service dinner in Reno I'm planning to attend. It's a retirement party for the forest supervisor. We're all expected to be there. A fancy dinner. Kind of a dressy affair."

"That sounds nice." Oh, she didn't like the sound of this. She could feel it coming and knew she wouldn't like the outcome.

"And I was wondering if you'd accompany me," he said.

Her brain screeched to a halt, and she stared at him, dumbfounded. Blinking. Her mind vacant. Here it was. And now what?

He hurried on, as if he feared she might say no. "Everyone will be there from the Forest Service. The entire hotshot crew, everyone. You probably already know most of them. It's just that I hate going to this kind of stuff alone."

Oh, this didn't sound good. She couldn't go with him. Absolutely not. She'd attended a number of these events with Blaine, but she had no intention of going as Jared's date. Seeing old acquaintances she'd known back when her husband had still been alive. Chatting as though nothing bad had ever happened. And now, she was going with the new FMO? That was bound to cause some gossip. No, she just couldn't.

"It'd be a huge favor to me," he said. "I'm still learning who everyone is and settling into my new job. Since you already know so many people, I thought it'd make things easier if you accompanied me. Besides, Sean and Connie and everyone else from my office are determined to hook me up, and I'm not really interested in dating right now."

Neither was she. After all, she could never replace Blaine. Not in a zillion years. But she did owe Jared for his kindness. He'd done so much for her family already.

"It'd be a huge favor, if you'd say yes," he said.

A favor for a friend.

"So this isn't really a date, but rather you're just trying to scare off the vultures, right?" she said.

He laughed. "Right. That's one way of looking at it. No date. Just friends. Will you go with me? Please. I don't want any entanglements I might regret later on."

Hmm. It sounded as if he felt almost the same about dating as she did. And she did owe him. Big-time. For fixing her washing machine and swing, not to mention lending her his truck and saving June's life. Maybe this was a way she could repay his generosity.

His blue eyes met hers, and she could see the intense beseeching written on his face. He looked desperate and earnest, silently begging her to say yes.

"Well, if it'll help keep you from getting stuck on a blind date, I guess it would be okay just this once."

He released a whoosh of air, as though he'd

been holding his breath. "Really? You mean it? You'll accompany me?"

Oh, she was going to regret this. She just knew it. But she plunged ahead anyway. "Sure. I think I can make some arrangements for the kids. Which night is it?"

He exhaled a giant sigh, as though he were mightily relieved. Within a few moments, he'd given her the particulars and set up the time for him to pick her up.

"We'll have to leave an hour early, so we have time to drive into Reno. And I'll get you home quite late. You know how these Forest Service parties go. Will that be okay?" he asked.

"Sure. The hazard pay we made on the last fire allowed me to hire a new waitress and a cook to work part-time. The cook is very reliable. I'll ask her to close the restaurant that evening for me. We should be covered," she said.

He flashed a smile so bright that she had to blink. And suddenly, she was excited by this opportunity. More and more, she seemed to be arranging for other people to cover the restaurant for her. To have some time to breathe. This would be a fun treat. Getting away for a while. Chatting with old friends she hadn't seen since Blaine's death. Maybe it was time for her to get out more.

"Thanks, Meg. I'll owe you big-time for this one."

Meg. The last person to call her that name had been her husband. Hearing it again made her feel all warm and bubbly inside. And she reminded herself that this was not a date. It was simply a business function. It meant nothing. Just a regular night out. She was helping Jared meet his obligations without becoming entangled in a relationship neither of them wanted. It couldn't do either of them any harm. Could it?

Chapter Nine

Megan stood in front of the mirror, putting on her dangly earrings. The ones that matched her blue beaded evening gown. She ran her hands over the long, silky skirt, happy that she could still fit in this dress. It'd been a long time since she'd put it on, and she barely recognized herself. She seemed like another person, her dress so different from the blue jeans, shirts and tennis shoes she normally wore every day.

She'd applied an extra bit of mascara and eye shadow, a pinch of color to her cheeks, and topped her makeup off with a hint of glossy color on her lips. She'd pinned her hair up on one side, leaving the reddish-blond curls to pour over her left shoulder. She couldn't remember the last time she'd dressed up for a fancy date.

Correction. Not a date. A favor. She was just helping out a friend. Saving Jared from all the matchmakers who would be milling around the forest supervisor's retirement party. She kept reminding herself of that fact.

So why did it feel like a date?

"You look nice, Mommy." June sat on the edge of the bed in Megan's room.

"Thanks, honey." Megan spritzed a bit of perfume on her neck. Not too much but just enough. Although this wasn't a real date, she still felt pretty and feminine. Which was refreshing, since she usually felt harried and dowdy.

"Are you gonna dance at the party?" June asked, adjusting her position so that she lay on her stomach, her elbows bent so she could rest her chin in her hands.

"Possibly."

"With Jared?"

Megan froze. Turning, she looked at her daughter. A troubled frown tugged at the girl's high forehead. Megan realized she hadn't thought this through. Nor had she fully considered how it might impact her children.

"I probably won't dance," she said as she

sat on one corner of the bed and rubbed June's back.

"You should," June said. "Jared likes you, Mom."

Megan took a settling breath. "That's because we're friends."

"Is he gonna be my new daddy?" June asked.

Whoa! How had she gone from doing a favor to marrying the guy? Megan was stunned that her daughter would even suggest it. But it was an indicator of why June had held such animosity toward Jared. She felt threatened and thought he was trying to take her father's place.

"No, honey. We're just friends. And even if I do eventually remarry, no one will ever take your father's place. Your daddy will always be ours, until the end of time."

"Yeah, that's what Jared said, too."

Megan inclined her head, surprised by this news. "He did? When?"

"A while back when he had dinner at the restaurant with Caleb and me."

A warm feeling blanketed Megan, yet she didn't want to discuss the topic. She knew Jared must mean well. That he was trying to be considerate of their feelings. But it surprised her that he'd discussed her husband with her kids. "We're friends and nothing more."

"So you don't want to marry Jared?" June asked.

Megan shook her head. "No, I don't. Not at all."

June sat up. "Why not?"

Here it was. She had to voice her feelings out loud, because there was no getting around the truth.

"Because he's a firefighter, and I think that's a dangerous profession."

"Oh." June's forehead knitted in deep thought. She looked so grown-up for all her young years. "You're afraid he might get killed like Daddy?"

Megan nodded helplessly. Of all the people she should confide her deepest fear to, she'd never expected it to be her eight-year-old daughter.

June leaned forward and hugged her. "Don't worry, Mommy. God will take care of us. Everything will work out for the best."

Tears burned Megan's eyes and she blinked. Her daughter's faith astounded her. Megan had spoken these words to her children on numerous occasions, yet she had said them more as a comfort thing. Now she had to search her heart and ask if she really believed it.

"Jared's a nice man," June said. "I don't mind if you go out with him."

Megan smiled. Ever since Jared had rescued June from the fallen tent, the girl had changed toward the man. "How did you get to be so smart?"

June shrugged. "I read a lot."

Megan laughed, then kissed the top of June's head. "I love you, sweetheart."

"I love you, too," June said.

Megan stood and slipped on her high heels, but a nagging suspicion nibbled at the back of her mind. She knew all too well that friendship between a man and a woman could soon blossom into something deeper. In fact, her mother had advised her years ago that she should marry her best friend. In college, that's what Blaine had been. Her best friend. And that's what frightened Megan the most. Friends was okay, but her relationship with Jared couldn't go further than that. It just couldn't.

"Wow, Mommy. You sure look pretty." Caleb stood in the doorway to her bedroom, his eyes round and glowing.

Megan hugged her son. "Thank you, darling."

"Can't I come with you?" Caleb asked.

"No, silly." June nudged his shoulder. "Mom's going on a date with Jared."

The boy screwed his nose up in disgust. "So? Why can't I come, too?"

"Because it's a date. They might want to hug and smooch and stuff like that," June insisted.

Caleb looked at his mother. "You want to hug and smooch Jared?"

Megan bit back a gasp of surprise. "No, honey. It's not a real date. Jared and I are just friends. We're just going to this retirement party together."

Caleb tilted his head in confusion, but the doorbell rang, shutting off any more explanations.

"I'll get it." The little boy ran toward the living room with June hot on his heels.

Megan picked up her clutch purse and followed, walking slow on her skyscraper heels.

"Hi, Emily." Caleb hugged the babysitter.

"Hi, buddy." Emily ruffled the boy's hair.

"Mom got pizza for us," June said.

"She did, huh?" Emily looked at Megan.

"Yes, there are several in the freezer. You'll have to bake one for each kid, and then whatever you like." Megan gestured toward the kitchen.

Pizza in a town this size consisted of homemade or frozen from the grocery store. There were no pizza parlors available. Caleb had chosen a frozen pepperoni and cheese, while June had asked for a Hawaiian.

Caleb reached for a DVD and held it up for Emily to see. A Disney movie he'd watched at least six times before. "Can we watch this one tonight?"

Emily nodded. "Sure, whatever you like."

"Mom's going out with Jared, but it's not a real date and she doesn't want to smooch him," Caleb said.

Megan just shook her head. She would have laughed if it weren't so serious.

"Hi there."

They all turned. Jared stood in the open doorway, holding a bouquet of yellow roses and baby's breath wrapped in green tissue paper in one hand and a single yellow rose in his other hand. Oh, boy. If this wasn't a real date, it sure felt like it.

"Hi, Jared. We're gonna eat pizza and popcorn while you're not on a date with Mom." Caleb hopped up and down in his stocking feet.

Megan's face flooded with heat. She definitely should have explained a bit more to her kids. But she figured any more talking about the subject would only make things worse.

Jared smiled and glanced at Megan. "You are, huh? That sounds fun."

He held out the single yellow rose to June. "This is for you, sweetheart."

The girl blinked in awe. She reached out tentatively and took the rose, as if it was fragile and might break. "No one ever gave me a flower before."

"Well, I'm glad to be the first, then," he said.

She tilted her head and looked up at him with shy eyes. And when she spoke, her voice sounded rather timid. "Thank you."

"You're welcome. Are you doing okay?" he asked, and they each understood his question. The tent mishap had been upsetting for all of them, especially June.

"Yes, I'm fine. How about you?" The shyness was gone as she gazed at his chin.

He gestured to his wound, where a small pink line showed where the stitches had been removed. "I'm great, but do you think the scar is too noticeable?"

June shook her head. "No, you can't hardly even tell."

Both he and June smiled, and Megan knew the two had become friends.

"And these are for you." Jared turned and held the bouquet out to Megan.

He looked achingly handsome in a pin-striped suit, red paisley tie and shiny black wingtip shoes. So formal in comparison to his Forest Service uniform. He'd slicked his dark blond hair back, his face freshly shaven. And he smelled very nice. In a rush, Megan felt a moment of absolute panic sweep over her.

He looked good. Too good. And she realized how much she missed the company of a handsome man.

This isn't a date. This isn't a date. She kept repeating the words over and over inside her mind.

His gaze swept over her attire with approval. "You look absolutely stunning tonight," he said, snapping her out of her thoughts.

Oh, that didn't help matters. In fact, his words made her feel weak in the knees.

"Thank you. You look nice, too."

Sudden warmth flushed across her face. She took the roses, her fingers brushing against his as they wrapped around the green tissue. She felt an electric zap of awareness that left her disconcerted and uneasy. This no longer felt like just a favor for a friend. In fact, she wasn't sure what it felt like.

"Thank you. That's so kind of you. I'll put them in some water," she said.

Carrying the flowers, she shifted into autopilot and walked into the kitchen to find a vase. Sandy followed, opening the fridge to peer inside, then the cupboard, to get out a pan to cook the pizzas on. "You're really lucky, Mrs. Rocklin," the girl whispered.

"Oh, how's that?"

"He's romantic—and really hot!" She flashed a wide, knowing smile and jerked her head toward Jared.

Megan rested one hand on the counter and released a steadying breath. She agreed with Emily—though she wouldn't tell her so. But Megan would have to be half-dead not to notice Jared's dynamic good looks.

"That's my daddy." Caleb's voice came from the living room.

Megan glanced over her shoulder. Her children were gazing up at a picture sitting on the fireplace mantel. It showed Megan and Blaine on their wedding day, dressed in their beautiful white clothes, smiling and happy.

"It is, huh?" Jared peered at the picture. "Your dad was a handsome guy," he said, looking down at June.

"He was the most handsome man in the whole wide world," the little girl said with conviction.

Megan's throat tightened. She didn't want

to discuss her husband with another man. But she liked the loyalty her children had for their father. And then, she felt a humbling gratitude that God had led her to Blaine. All her life, she'd wanted to marry a good man and give her children the best father she could. She believed she had done that with Blaine. But now, she wondered if lightning could strike in the same place twice. Was it possible for her to ever find two such wonderful men? If so, she'd be truly blessed. But it couldn't be Jared. Her heart couldn't risk losing another man the way she'd lost Blaine. She needed to fall for someone who wasn't a firefighter. Someone with a safe, boring job.

"Well, we better be on our way." She retrieved a delicate sweater from the coat closet, then picked up her purse.

Jared's eyes met hers. "You all ready?"

She nodded. As he opened the door, her heart was beating like a bass drum. She stumbled and he clasped her arm, steadying her. The warmth of his fingers sent tingles shooting up her arm.

"You okay?"

She gave a nervous laugh. "Yes, thank you. Sorry to be so clumsy. I'm not used to wearing high heels."

"I know you ladies like to wear those skyscrapers on your feet, but if it helps, you look really nice tonight."

Yes, it helped. At least he'd noticed. But then she wondered why she'd taken such great care with her appearance. It didn't matter. Did it?

He held her arm as they walked toward the driveway, where he opened her door and helped her step up into his truck. A round decal just below the window caught her eye. A picture of Smokey the Bear pointing a warning finger at her with the words Only You Can Prevent Forest Fires.

Another vivid reminder of what Jared did for a living.

"Careful there. We've got an hour-and-a-half drive ahead of us, so you can kick off your shoes and relax for a while."

She smiled her gratitude and clicked on her seat belt. As he climbed into the truck, turned the key and backed away from her house, she glanced over and saw her two children and Emily with their noses pressed up against the windowpane. She returned Caleb's wave, feeling edgy and nervous. As though she were going to the executioner's block.

The low rumble of the engine sounded comforting yet set her on edge. This evening was a reminder of how lonely she'd been this past year. And she realized Jared was wreaking havoc on her well-ordered world.

"Are you warm enough?"

At Jared's question, Megan glanced up. He gripped the steering wheel with his hands, looking straight ahead. Although this wasn't a real date, he still felt kind of nervous. Afternoon sunlight blazed against the black asphalt. Soon, it would be dark. Jared barely noticed the scenery of the town whisking by as they turned onto the freeway.

"Yes, in fact I'm a bit hot," she said.

He reached over and adjusted a knob on the dashboard. A whoosh of cool air brushed against his cheek.

"Is that better?" he asked.

"Yes, thank you." She folded her hands primly in her lap.

"Do you own a car, or just a truck?" she asked.

"Just a truck. I've always been a truck kind of guy. What about you?" He was trying to make conversation, and this seemed like a safe topic. The ride into Reno gave them lots of time to chat.

"We had a car once, before my husband died. I drove it most of the time, because I always had the kids with me."

He glanced over at her. "But no more? Why'd you get rid of it?"

"It was pretty old, and I couldn't afford to keep both vehicles. I sold the car and kept the truck, thinking it'd be more helpful with running the restaurant. Sometimes I have to drive into Reno for supplies."

He nodded. "Sounds logical, but your kids seem to do okay in the truck."

"Do you have kids?"

He coughed, her question taking him off guard. A pinch of regret tweaked his heart. "I'm afraid not. I always wanted children, but my wife didn't like them. She said she didn't want any *little monsters* making messes or ruining her silk blouses."

"Did you know that when you married her?"

No, he hadn't.

"Unfortunately, she changed her mind about having a family after we married. We got hitched right out of college. I tried to be what she wanted, but I wasn't enough. I was working long hours. Living in such small towns, she got bored. I think that's what helped lead to her infidelity."

Megan flinched. "Oh, Jared. I'm so sorry."

"It's okay. She liked working out and keeping her tiny figure. Looking good was of high importance to her. She didn't want any kids to give her stretch marks."

Megan chuckled. "Well, kids definitely do make messes. They also grow up to be some of the most amazing people in the world. But what got you and your wife together in the first place?"

He adjusted the rearview mirror. Anything to distract himself from this conversation. He really didn't want to talk about this, but he also wouldn't avoid Megan's earnest questions. "During college, Sharon was a different person. She was carefree and happy and easy to be with. After we graduated and got married, she wanted me to work in her father's bank. But that's not what I wanted. She knew I was studying to be a fire scientist. I'd always planned to work for the Forest Service, but she never accepted that. She thought fighting fires was a hobby, not a full-time career. Over time, she came to resent me for it."

And before he knew what he was doing, he'd told Megan everything. How Sharon had kept putting off having a family and had finally told him that she didn't want kids at all.

"The surprising thing is that I found out several months ago that she's now expecting a child with her new husband," he said.

"That must have been so difficult for you," Megan said.

He heard the sincerity in her voice but no pity. And he was grateful for that. A hard lump clogged his throat and he tried to swallow.

"It was. I can't help wondering what's wrong with me. Why I couldn't make her happy. But what hurts the most isn't that she didn't want kids, but that she didn't want to have them with me," he said.

"I doubt that's true. It sounds like she didn't know what she wanted," Megan said in a kind tone.

He gave an acerbic laugh, still feeling betrayed and bitter after all this time. "Maybe so. I'm sorry. I didn't mean to be a downer tonight."

"No, it's okay," she said. "I understand that you've been hurt."

But he'd confided something he hadn't told another living person. And he realized that Megan was way too easy to talk to. Though they weren't romantically involved, he felt a kinship with this woman that he didn't understand. In spite of their reticence, they'd become good friends.

"Actually, it kind of feels good to finally talk about it," he said. "For so long, I've kept it all bottled up inside. I thought I'd gotten over it, but maybe not. In retrospect, I didn't realize until too late that my wife and I weren't compatible. Even though she hated my work, I loved it and have never regretted it."

Megan released a pensive sigh, and he realized that she understood. And that somehow brought them closer together. He couldn't explain why, but he felt as if he could trust Megan. That she was genuine and would never betray him.

"And what about you?" He met her gaze. Her expressive eyes seemed to search deep inside of him, and he had to look away.

She lifted one shoulder. "What about me?"

"Tell me about your husband."

"Talk about blunt." She laughed, but it sounded cold and hollow.

"I'm sorry, but I'd really like to know some more about him."

She took a deep breath and let it go. "We met in college, too. He was in a forestry program, and I was going to culinary school. His profession was much like yours. I always knew we'd live in small towns. It kind of goes with working for the Forest Service. Like you, he always worked on a fire crew during the summer months, to pay his school tuition in the fall. Then, right out of college, he joined the Minoa hotshot crew and hoped to one day work his way up to becoming the superintendent. I was raised in small towns, so I never minded his work, until he got killed. Then I didn't..."

She trailed off, as though she couldn't speak the words. But he knew. She'd lost her husband in a wildfire and that must have soured her on the profession. He couldn't really blame her.

"Likewise, I'm sorry to make you rehash painful memories," he said with an understanding smile. "I'm sure it hasn't been easy, losing your husband and raising two kids on your own."

"No, it hasn't. And yet, I have a lot to be grateful for."

"Me, too. But how'd you end up owning the restaurant?"

She gripped the armrest and gazed out at the scenery as it flashed by. "My father-in-law owned it. My husband grew up working in the diner, just like I'm raising my kids. When his dad passed away a few years ago, he left the restaurant to us. I was already working there as a cook, so it seemed natural for me to just step in and run the place. In retrospect, it was a blessing. It gave me a livelihood after...after Blaine died."

"You have two wonderful kids," he said.

"Yes, they're great, aren't they?"

He smiled, liking the way her eyes sparkled when she talked about her children. She was a good mother. "The best. And I even think June is starting to like me."

"She is. She's just very cautious," Megan said.

"And probably still missing her dad."

Megan inclined her head. "Yes. I worry about both of them."

"Why is that?"

"Because I'm so busy. I'm working at the restaurant all the time. I'd send the kids to a child care provider more frequently, but then I'd never get to see them. Thankfully, they're pretty well behaved most of the time, so I bring them with me when I can."

"Don't be so hard on yourself," he said. "I think your kids are exceptional. They mind you very well, have good manners, and seem inquisitive and happy. You've done a great job with them."

She smiled her thanks, and the warmth of happiness filled his chest. He liked the way this woman made him feel better about himself. He had a lot to be grateful for. He was making new friends and had a thriving career. All he was missing was someone to share his life with. Someone to confide all his hopes and dreams to.

Someone to love.

"I envy you that," he said.

"You mean my children?"

He nodded. "Yeah, I always wanted kids. Now I may never get the chance."

His heart gave a hard pinch. Without a wife and family of his own, he felt as though he were missing out on a vital part of life. He didn't want to be alone, but he didn't want to be hurt again, either.

"I'm sure you'll marry again. You'll have children one day," she said.

He released a heavy sigh. "I'm not so sure."

And suddenly, he didn't want to talk about this anymore. It hurt too much. For so long, he'd pushed everyone away. Any woman that had gotten too close, he feared they might break his heart again. He hadn't even considered dating or being with another woman.

Until recently.

"I have to put in an appearance at the retirement party tonight, but when you've had enough, you just let me know and we'll leave. We don't have to stay all evening," he said.

"Okay, thanks."

The topic of discussion changed, and by

the time they arrived in Reno, Jared felt as though he'd known this woman all his life.

They pulled into valet parking. Stars glittered in the sky. Darkness gathered around them, and he saw Megan shiver. Handing his keys over to the attendant who would park his truck, Jared smoothed Megan's sweater over her shoulders. He took her arm and politely escorted her into the party. Although he smiled and chatted with her, a heavy sadness settled over him. The conviction that he might never get a second chance at love. And as much as he hated the thought of being hurt again, nothing frightened him more than living the rest of his life all alone.

Chapter Ten

As Jared accompanied Megan into the retirement party, she felt his fingertips resting lightly on her back. A simple gesture. Polite and considerate. Not really territorial. And yet, it branded them as a couple.

They paused in the outer foyer, and she stepped away, trying not to appear obvious in her efforts to put some distance between them. Music filtered over the air along with the low hum of happy chatter. People clustered together, laughing and sipping from their glasses. Megan recognized a couple of them and couldn't help feeling a tad jittery. Even if this wasn't a real date, she was still here with Jared. She was his date for the night in deed, if not in name.

"Jared! How are you?"

A burly, sweaty man greeted them at the door.

"Hi, Sam," Jared said with a half smile.

"And Megan Rocklin. Well, I'll be. You're looking good." Sam swayed slightly, smelling of heavy liquor.

Megan wasn't surprised. Sam worked on a pumper truck crew. He was good at his job and normally kind and gregarious. But every time they had a company party like this, he got mean, rotten drunk. And right now, Megan wanted to avoid the guy.

"Hello." Without thinking about it, she sidled closer to Jared. Only afterward did she recognize what she'd done and that it was an unconscious effort to maintain safety. But why she would evade Sam by seeking Jared's silent protection was beyond her. It didn't seem right, and yet it felt so natural.

Sam glanced between the two of them and staggered. Although the evening was early, he was obviously inebriated and slurred his words. "Did you two come here together?"

Jared rested his hand on Megan's arm, and she took comfort from his presence. "Yes, as a matter of fact, we did."

Sam lifted his glass to Megan and grinned. "Well, let's see. Blaine's been dead about a year now. So, off with the old and on with the new, right?"

Megan tensed. A hard lump rose in her throat, and she felt as though her heart had dropped to her stomach. Out of her peripheral vision, she caught Jared's tight expression. He didn't like this situation, either. She didn't fight him when he deftly pulled her around and placed himself at the fore.

"Excuse us, will you?" Jared said.

He didn't wait for Sam's response but led Megan into the ballroom. Sam's barking laughter grated behind them, but Jared kept on going. Megan followed right behind, grateful to get away.

"I'm sorry about that," Jared whispered for her ears alone as they stood in the doorway and took in the lay of the land.

Yeah, she was, too. She knew this was a bad idea to come here with Jared. Everyone might be thinking the same thing. That she'd forgotten all about Blaine. That she was ready to move on. But she wasn't. Not at all.

"It's all right. But thanks for getting us out of there." Her body was trembling as she pulled away from him to greet several Minoa hotshots. Good old friends she could rely on. Megan was grateful to see them but wondered for the umpteenth time if coming here tonight was a mistake.

"Hi, Megan." Tessa hailed her with a wave of her hand.

Megan immediately hugged the other woman. "Tessa! It's so good to see a friendly face."

After a moment, Tessa drew back and brushed her fingertips against the dainty beads on Megan's dress. "This is lovely. You sure look nice tonight. Doesn't she, Jared?"

Standing close by, he cleared his throat and nodded. "Absolutely stunning."

Megan's face flushed with heat. His praise pleased her enormously. "Thanks, both of you. And your dress is beautiful, too."

Megan admired Tessa's black silk and smiled, trying to be pleasant.

Tessa brushed a hand against the shimmery skirt of her gown. "It's quite different from the usual garb I wear, right?"

Megan nodded. "Definitely. I'm used to seeing you in your work boots and yellow Nomex fire shirt."

The two women laughed.

Megan jerked when Zach swept up behind them and put his arms around both ladies. "Hey, you two. Tonight should be fun. I see lots of beautiful women here, present company at the top of the list."

Tessa swatted playfully at her brother. "Just because you didn't bring a date doesn't give you an excuse to latch onto us. We're taken, so you can't misbehave."

"I never misbehave. Much," he snickered.

Dressed in a suit and no tie, Zach looked rather casual compared to Jared and the other men in the room. But his boyish smile was so open and friendly that Megan figured the guy could get away with almost anything. Zach was handsome and laid-back, and Megan couldn't understand why he didn't have a dozen babes following him everywhere. It was only a matter of time before some sweet young lady latched on to him.

Ignoring her brother, Tessa leaned closer to Megan. "Sean told me Jared was bringing a date tonight, and I hoped it was you. I'm so glad to see you out again. Now, if we can just set this guy up with some girl, our problems would be solved." She jerked a thumb at her brother.

Zach opened his arms wide, an innocent expression on his face. "What can I say? You can't mess with perfection. But I'll find someone one day. I'm patient."

"And the sooner, the better," Tessa teased.

Zach pulled his sister close for a tight hug and kissed her on the cheek as he tickled her ribs. "Ah, you love me, sis. Admit it."

Tessa chuckled, but Megan just smiled at their antics. They were fun and easy to be around, and it felt so natural. As though she belonged here—with Jared by her side. Did her comfort with this man and the other hotshots mean she was being disloyal to Blaine?

"Sean is over there. Come and sit with us," Tessa suggested, bringing Megan out of her thoughts. Tessa indicated a table near the dance floor, where Sean was sitting in deep conversation with Brian Dandridge.

"Yeah, Tim and Connie are at our table, too. We should be a happy crowd tonight," Zach said.

As they headed over, Jared and Megan were engulfed by coworkers and their spouses. Employees from the regional office were there, too, everyone catching up on old news and sharing a laugh or two. Both Jared and Megan had to fend off inquiries as to how serious their relationship was.

"Well, Jared Marshall. It's been years." A tall, raw-boned man with a headful of shocking red hair smiled and thrust out a hand.

"Walt Hampton. How are you doing?" Jared shook the man's hand.

"I'm good. And you?"

"The same." Jared introduced Megan to the man.

Walt eyed her curled hairdo. "Why, she's lovely, Jared. You found a beauty, that's for sure."

Megan smiled, feeling charmed by the man's words. "Thank you."

Walt took her hand and leaned near. "I worked with Jared in Colorado. Back then, he was married to that harpy, Sharon. I'm sure glad to see he's got someone better now. He deserves to be happy."

Megan's face flooded with heat. The mention of Jared's ex-wife felt too personal, especially after what he'd told her on their drive into Reno. She'd heard the hurt in his voice when he'd said that Sharon didn't want his children. And for some odd reason, it made Megan angry at the woman. Jared was a nice man. He deserved to be happily married. He deserved to be a father.

"Megan and I are just friends, Walt," Jared said.

Walt slapped him on the back. "Sure you are. That's how all the best marriages start out. With friendship."

Megan blinked, realizing Walt was right.

But this was one friendship that would never progress to romance. She would see to that.

They talked a few minutes more, then got interrupted by someone else. Jared spent most of his time deflecting personal questions and innuendos. Not once did Megan lose her composure. She tried to face it all with grace and charm, but inside, she was a nervous wreck.

Finally they were asked to sit down for dinner. Gratefully, Megan headed for her seat. As they walked to their table, Jared rested his hand at the small of her back. She was once again surprised by the intimacy of the gesture. It'd been a long time since a man had been solicitous of her. She was conflicted and couldn't make sense of her emotions tonight.

"Does it feel odd to be here with me tonight?" Jared asked Megan quietly as they ate their roasted chicken.

"A little," she confessed.

She glanced up and caught several people looking at them, their heads bent close together as though they were discussing them.

"How are you holding up?" he said.

"I'm fine. I knew what I might be getting myself into when I agreed to come here with you. It's okay. Stop worrying. I'm fine."

"That's a very kind answer. You're a spirited lady, and I appreciate you being here," he said.

Before Megan could digest his words, he reached out and squeezed her hand. The contact was electric. Nor did it go unnoticed by Connie. A warm glow filled the woman's eyes, but she didn't say anything. Thank goodness.

Megan pulled her hand away and clutched her fingers together in her lap.

The assistant forest supervisor stood up at the podium and tapped the microphone to get their attention.

"Good evening, everyone. We're glad you all could make it out tonight."

He went on to welcome Jim Gardner, the forest supervisor and guest of honor. Jim sat with his wife at the front table and smiled. A number of people took the mic and made jokes at Jim's expense. They dimmed the lights and showed a slide presentation that included Jim getting dumped in the creek, supervising a forest fire and other various activities from his career with the Forest Service. One slide flashed overhead showing Jim at a parade. He stood on the back of a Forest Service pumper truck. A handsome young man stood next to him, wearing a Smokey the

Bear outfit, holding the bear head beneath his arm as he smiled wide for the camera.

Megan gave a little gasp.

"Are you okay?" Jared whispered.

Megan didn't answer. She gripped folds of her dress and bit her bottom lip. The man standing next to the forest supervisor was Blaine.

No one else seemed to think much of it as the next slide flashed onto the screen, but Megan felt a coldness sweep over her. She sat very still and quiet. Smiling and nodding at the appropriate times. Polite and reasonable. But it still hurt. She couldn't help but feel the pain of losing her husband again and again. She'd let down her guard, and then Blaine had appeared out of nowhere on the screen. A constant reminder of all that Megan and her children had lost. A reminder that she should never have agreed to come here tonight.

As soon as the slide presentation was over with, they said some hasty farewells and Jared whisked her out of there. He seemed to know that she'd had enough for one evening. Megan was beyond grateful for his considerate insight. The last thing she wanted to do was wait until everyone was leaving and be put through another barrage of questions and innuendos.

They stood silently outside, waiting for the valet to retrieve Jared's vehicle. Megan folded her arms and huddled beneath her light sweater. She felt lost and forlorn. No longer comfortable and happy to be here.

A few minutes later, they were inside Jared's truck. He flipped on the headlights and pulled away from the convention center. The whoosh of warm air from the heater filled the void.

"I'm sorry, Megan."

She didn't look at him. "For what?"

"For bringing you here. I know some people made some foolish comments tonight, yet you seemed very accepting," he said.

"Don't be. People ask stupid questions all the time, but I don't think they meant any harm. They knew Blaine. His work was a big part of his life. It hurts to think of him being gone, but I can't begrudge reminders of him. Besides, it was time to get out and show people that I'm still alive." She glanced his way, trying to believe what she said. But in her heart of hearts, she was in shock and wanted nothing more than to run away.

"I saw the picture of Blaine in the Smokey the Bear costume," Jared said.

Megan laughed, but it sounded hollow to her ears. "Yes, he loved parades. I've got a cute picture of him wearing the bear costume and holding both of our kids in his arms. Now and then, I get it out and show it to June and Caleb. They love it. I don't want to forget him. Not ever. So, I was glad to see his picture there tonight, doing what he loved."

She was trying to convince herself she was really fine with everything, but her body trembled with the loss. She figured it was part of the grieving process. Something she had to deal with. On the one hand, it was good to see that her beloved husband hadn't been forgotten, but it was also sad and difficult to think of him never coming back. It was hard to move on without him, but she realized she had to.

"You have an amazing perspective," Jared said.

She gave a croaking laugh. "Not really. Don't get me wrong. Losing Blaine still hurts. A lot. But I'm also happy to know he isn't forgotten by everyone, least of all me and his kids."

Jared didn't know what to say. He didn't regret this evening—for the most part he'd had a wonderful time. But he also felt dumb and foolish. Because no matter how much he kept telling himself he wasn't looking for love, deep inside, he wished Megan could make room in her heart for him. And from what she'd just said, maybe she could never let go of Blaine, and Jared didn't stand a chance with her.

He couldn't compete with the memory of her dead husband, and he didn't want a repeat of what had happened with his ex-wife. He would never marry again, unless he was positive the woman loved him unconditionally for who he was and not for what she wanted him to be.

Yet despite all that, was he crazy to want something to happen between them? The only way to see if it might work between them was to put himself forward and find out. It would take a giant leap of trust, but he realized he had to take it or live forever with his regrets.

Megan didn't speak again for quite a while, and they settled into a comfortable silence. Both of them seemed lost in their own thoughts. By the time Jared dropped her off at her house, it was late. The porch light was on, the house dark.

Killing the engine, Jared hopped out of the truck and walked around to open Megan's door for her. He escorted her up to her front porch. Standing on the second step, she paused there, meeting his eyes. The pale moonlight bathed her beautiful face in golden light. He felt mesmerized. Lost in the beauty of her dark eyes.

He stepped closer, and it was a few moments before he realized that he'd taken her into his arms. She didn't pull away as he kissed her. Softly. A light caress. For a few profound seconds, she melted against his chest, pliant in his arms. Then she stiffened and pulled away.

"Jared, I can't." She glanced at him as though he were a mirage and she couldn't remember how she got here.

Jared almost groaned out loud. She'd just told him that she would never forget her husband, but he'd kissed her anyway. Stupid thing to do. And he wouldn't be surprised if she never spoke to him again.

"I'm sorry, Megan. I guess I violated the terms of our no-date agreement."

He stepped back, feeling awkward. He'd forgotten who he was and who she was and what they'd both been through. For a few blissful hours, he knew Megan had been happy and enjoyed herself. And he'd been happy as well, able to forget the heartache of his past. But now, it all came rushing back like a drenching rain.

She murmured something indistinct beneath her breath. A mingled sound of embarrassment and appeasement.

"I better get inside now," she said.

She turned to leave. He thought he should just shut up, turn around and get inside his truck and leave. But something held him in place. Something he didn't understand. He'd caught numerous glimpses of what it could be like with Megan. A glimpse of happiness. Maybe, just maybe…

"Megan," he called to her, and she turned. "Yes?"

He took a deep breath to settle his nerves. To give him courage for what he was about to do. "How would you and the kids like to go with me to the park next Monday evening?" he asked quickly, before he lost the courage.

She lifted her brows in a wary frown. "The park?"

"Yeah, with me."

She tensed. He knew she was taken off guard by his question. That she didn't necessarily like it.

"Um, I don't think so."

His heart dropped. For a flickering moment, a lance of pain filled his chest. He knew he shouldn't take her rejection personally, but he couldn't seem to help it. He hunched his shoulders and slid his hands into his pants pockets.

She looked at him, and he saw something in her eyes. A look of empathy and regret. As though she could see inside of him and understood the sadness he felt there.

"Would…would it just be you, me and my kids?" she asked. "No other firefighters will be there with us?"

"No, it'd just be us."

"What did you have in mind?" she said.

A spark flickered inside of him. "I thought we'd have a picnic in the park. There wouldn't be anyone else there to deal with. Just us having fun together."

He held his breath, wanting her to say yes, but hoping she made it easier on both of them and said no. It was just the park, after all. Not much could happen with her kids tagging along. And yet, he wasn't sure he was up to this. It'd taken a ton of courage just to ask her out. But now, he didn't know if he wanted this.

"Hmm. I've never been on a date with my kids before," she said.

He chuckled. "Well, I've got a surprise for them. Someone I'd like them to meet. If you'll trust me, I think they'll like it a lot."

"So, someone else is coming along with us, too?"

He lifted one shoulder. "Kind of, but it's not a person. It'll be fun. No pressure. Just a simple outing."

"I don't know." Her breath left her in a rush. He could tell she wanted to say yes, but something held her back. As though if she said yes, she'd be rowing out into the middle of the Atlantic Ocean and throwing away both oars.

"I'll bring the picnic. You don't need to worry about a thing except showing up. You'll have a night off from cooking. Just come and have a fun time," he urged, gaining more confidence. Hoping she'd say yes.

She hesitated.

"Don't worry," he hurried on. "Your children are gonna love it. Say yes."

He tried not to sound so desperate, but he really wanted her to go with him.

She waved a hand in the air and made a little sound of resignation. "Okay, but only if I can bring the dessert."

"Deal." He almost laughed with relief. Almost. He couldn't believe she'd agreed.

"Do you want to meet at the park?"

"Actually, would you mind coming over to my place at six o'clock? Then I can introduce the kids to that special someone I was telling you about. We can go to the park from there. Does that sound okay?"

"Sure."

"Just one warning. I'm not as good a cook as you are, but I think it'll be palatable," he said.

"I'm sure it will." She chuckled, and he was charmed by her beautiful smile.

"Okay, I'll see you then. Good night." He stepped off the porch.

"Good night." She spoke firmly as she reached for the doorknob.

As she slid inside and closed the door, he stood beside his truck, breathing hard. Wondering if he'd just made the biggest mistake of his life. He didn't want to lose his friendship with Megan, and yet he might not have a choice. Because he'd kissed her and had a glimpse of what their future together might look like. The lines between friendship and romance had just blurred. Big-time.

Chapter Eleven

This was a mistake. A big, bad mistake that Megan knew she would come to regret. When Jared had invited her and the kids for a picnic in the park, he'd looked so hopeful. And when she'd said no, she'd seen the crushing blow in his eyes. She had no doubt he'd felt rejected. And after what he'd told her about his ex-wife not wanting his children, Megan didn't have the heart to turn him down. No, she wanted to see him smile. To hear his laughter. To hear his deep, animated voice as they chatted about nothing and everything.

She parked her truck in front of Jared's framed house. White with forest green shutters. Afternoon sunlight glinted through the treetops. No flowers grew along the borders lining the house, but the bushes were groomed to perfection. The warmer weather meant longer days and a fresh scent of spring. It was a beautiful time of year, but she was always aware that any day now, they could get another wildfire.

Stepping out of her vehicle, Megan reached back inside to help June and Caleb hop down, then picked up the peach pie she'd made for dessert. Holding it tight, she pushed the door closed with her hip. Caleb took her free hand as they walked toward the house.

"Jared lives here?" he said in his overly loud voice.

"Yes, sweetheart."

"What are we gonna eat for dinner?" June asked, brushing her hand against the boxwoods lining the sidewalk leading up to Jared's front door.

"I don't know. He said he was making us a picnic, so I suspect we're going to eat in the park."

Caleb gave a little skip. "That sounds fun, huh, Mommy? I love picnics in the park."

"Me, too," June said.

Megan wanted to reserve judgment. She pushed the doorbell with her elbow and waited. Within a few moments, the door whooshed open and Jared greeted them.

"Hi there. Come on in." The man pushed

open the screen door and held it wide while Megan and the children stepped inside.

The house smelled of pine needles and furniture polish. A cream-colored sofa sat along one wall with a coffee table in front. Framed black-and-white prints hung on the walls, and a treadmill sat strategically placed to face the big-screen TV. Clean and sterile. The complete opposite of her busy home with its heavy dose of children's books, puzzles and toys. But she liked Jared's tidiness.

"Let me help you with that. It looks delicious." He didn't hesitate as he slid the pie out of her hands.

His quick gaze had her brushing a hand down the flower print of her sundress. He looked casual in cowboy boots and a white polo shirt tucked into the waist of his dark blue jeans. The collar of his shirt was open at the neck, and she had to force herself not to stare at the tanned flesh of his throat.

"Thank you," she said.

"Let's go out back for a few minutes." He led the way, pausing long enough to set the pie on the kitchen counter.

"I thought we were going over to the park for a picnic," June said.

"We are. But first, there's someone I'd like

you to meet." Jared slid the screen door open and waited for them to precede him outside.

A little golden puppy charged them the moment they stepped onto the green lawn.

"A dog!" Caleb gasped.

June squealed with joy and immediately went down on her hands and knees. "Oh, a sweet puppy."

The dog wriggled and squirmed, wagging its stubby tail. Its pink tongue lolled out of its mouth as it eagerly swarmed the kids.

Megan stared in surprise. "Is this your dog?"

"Yeah, I just got her last week. I thought the kids might like to meet her," Jared said.

"I've always wanted a dog," Caleb said, his face creased in an expression of joy.

"I know that. How about if you share this dog with me until you get your own?" Jared said.

"Really?" Both kids looked at him with awe.

"Of course. You can come over and visit her anytime you like."

"Oh, yes! That would be great. What's her name?" Caleb asked, closing his eyes as the puppy licked his face.

"Actually, I haven't named her yet. She's a golden retriever."

"Well, she's got to have a name, so she'll come when you call to her," June said in her grown-up voice.

Jared slid his hands into his pockets, a satisfied smile on his lips. "You are absolutely right. And I thought you might be able to help me out with that."

Caleb lifted his face, his mouth hanging open. "You mean we get to name her for you?"

"That's right. So what do you think we should call her?"

"How about Spot?" Caleb suggested.

"No, silly. She's got to have a spot on her fur to be named that. And this dog is too pretty for such an ugly name," June said.

The dog squirmed her way onto her lap, and the girl gave a happy giggle. "How about if we call her Sophie?"

Megan blinked, wondering where her daughter had come up with such a name. She would have expected Buster or Fluffy.

"Sophie's a pretty name," Caleb said.

Jared nodded. "It is. The name suits her quite well, I think. Sophie it is."

"Can we take her to the park with us on our picnic?" Caleb asked as he wrapped his arms around the little animal and hugged her tight.

"Of course. Since we'll be outdoors, I won't

have to worry about her having any accidents. I'm potty training her, so she has to go outside often." Jared stepped back. "Let's go. I've already got the picnic basket loaded in the back of my truck."

"Yay!" The kids cheered.

They stood and followed Jared toward the door, the puppy trotting happily at their feet.

Megan held back, feeling a bit overwhelmed by all of this. Honestly, she didn't know what to make of Jared and his dog. He seemed to have won her children's hearts so effortlessly, but she still had misgivings.

"Come on, Mom," Caleb called.

"I'll just get the pie." She hurried inside, picked up the pie, then made her way out to the driveway.

The kids were already loaded in the backseat of Jared's truck. He'd retrieved Caleb's booster seat from her truck and put it into his vehicle and was just finishing buckling the kids in before he handed them the puppy. They held the little dog between them on the seat. Sophie panted and wriggled, as happy as a dog could be. If Megan didn't know better, she would have thought Jared was a veteran parent. He seemed to know just what to do with her kids.

She didn't say much as Jared drove them to

the park, where they unloaded the pie and picnic basket. While the kids played in the grass with Sophie, Megan helped Jared spread a blanket for them to sit on. The Wilson family had just arrived with their three children. Bill, their father, was setting out their cooler chests beneath the gazebo by the barbecue pits. They waved hello and Megan lifted a hand, pasting a smile on her face.

Inwardly, Megan groaned. Susan Wilson had a big mouth. No doubt it'd be all over town by tomorrow that she'd been in the park having a picnic with Jared Marshall. But it was a little late to worry about people seeing them together.

"You're awfully quiet this evening," Jared said to her. "Is everything okay?"

No, it wasn't okay. She'd broken a promise to herself not to date a firefighter. And yet, she couldn't seem to help herself. It was as if she'd known this man for years. She wanted to be here, yet she didn't. She felt so conflicted, as though her heart were in a battle of tug-of-war.

"Yes, I'm just taking it all in. It's been a long time since I've seen my children this happy."

He jutted his chin toward them. Sophie was scampering around Caleb's feet, jumping up and barking. "A puppy and a picnic. It's an instant recipe for joy."

Yes, she had to agree. But when they both originated from the same man, she wondered if she was just asking for trouble.

"Caleb's been requesting a dog for months now. Except for the swing in our backyard, there's nothing he wants more."

Jared nodded. "I know. Little boys and dogs seem to go together."

"Yeah, maybe I'll have to get the kids a dog of their own."

"No rush. You can borrow Sophie anytime you like," he said.

They watched the kids play for a while longer.

"I envy your relationship with your husband," he said.

She angled her head to one side, his words taking her off guard. "And why is that?"

"Because you loved him."

"I think wives are supposed to love their husbands, and vice versa." They'd discussed this the other night, but she sensed he wasn't finished with the topic.

He nodded. "That's true, except I don't think my ex-wife ever loved me."

Megan arched one brow. "Not even in the beginning?"

"I thought so, but now I'm not so sure. I trusted her completely, and look where it got me."

Megan understood that concept quite well. She'd trusted Blaine, but he'd had no control over whether he was killed in a wildfire. It just happened. And against all her good common sense, she wanted to trust Jared, too.

He smiled. "That's why I accepted this new job here in Minoa. It was a chance to start over fresh. And I haven't regretted coming here."

"Well, you're probably better off. You deserve a happy life," she said.

Again, she knew she should keep her mouth shut. This wasn't her business, and she didn't want to ask too many questions.

He released a heavy sigh. "Yeah, I guess so. But you've had your share of sadness, too."

"Yes."

That's all she said. Memories swamped her. At first, she couldn't believe that Blaine was gone. They couldn't even see him, because he'd been burned so badly in the fire.

"I'm sorry, Megan." Jared's voice sounded low and heartfelt.

Maybe now was the time to be honest with him. To tell him how she really felt about firefighters. To put aside the facade and lay it all out on the line. "And that's why I…why I've promised never to love someone that fights fires or works in a dangerous profession again. It's nothing personal, Jared. But I just can't go through the pain of losing someone again."

There. She'd said the words. She'd put him on notice. Now they'd end their evening and she'd go home. And he'd never call her again. It was better this way. Better for Jared, too.

So why did she feel suddenly so lost and forlorn?

He went very still, his strong hands gripping a bottle of water. "Is there any way I can change your mind where I'm concerned?"

She looked down and swallowed hard. Since she'd met him, she'd felt nothing but a desire to be near him. To love and hold him close against her heart. But she didn't answer. She didn't need to. From the lengthening silence, she knew he'd gotten her message loud and clear.

"Well, at least you're being honest with me," he said.

She looked up. "I'm sorry, Jared. I don't mean to hurt your feelings. It's just that I've got two kids to worry about. I've got to put their needs first."

His eyes crinkled in a smile of understanding, but she saw the pain in his eyes. "Believe me, I understand. I just wish things could be different somehow."

And she realized in that moment that so did she. She tried to gather her thoughts, to take back what she'd said. But she couldn't. She had to tell him to go away and leave her alone. But honestly, that's not what she wanted. And she realized pushing this man away was getting more difficult every time she saw him.

Sophie barked and Jared glanced at the children. The little dog was growling and chewing on the hem of Caleb's blue jeans.

Jared laughed, breaking the tense moment. "I'm glad the kids like Sophie. They seem to be having a lot of fun."

Happy to change the topic, Megan didn't even look at the kids. Frankly, she couldn't take her eyes off Jared. "Why'd you decide to get a dog?"

He opened the lid to the basket and pulled out paper plates, a potato salad, fried chicken, sliced watermelon and a bag of potato chips. A perfect picnic. The afternoon sun glowed across the green expanse of the park, and she was grateful for the shade of a tall cottonwood tree.

"I thought it'd be fun to have a companion with me when I drive up into the mountains. Sophie will grow and get big. She'll be perfect for my line of work. I'm planning to train her to have manners, so she can go with me often."

Megan blinked, thinking he must be lonely, too. At least she had her children to enjoy, but Jared had no one. After what he'd told her about his divorce and having no children of his own, it was little wonder that he wanted a companion. Someone to be with. Someone to love.

"What will you do with Sophie when you go on a fire?" Megan asked.

"Connie said she'd watch her. She and Tim have a big backyard they can put the dog in. I just hope Sophie doesn't dig up Connie's petunias."

Megan laughed at that. "She better not. Connie might never forgive Sophie for that."

He laughed too, the sound deep and low.

Lifting her head, Megan gazed at her children. Their lilting voices rang throughout the air. Seeing the glowing happiness in their eyes, Megan went very still.

"Come and eat," Jared called to the kids.

They came running, and they all sat on the blanket and ate their dinner. Megan didn't speak much. Thankfully the kids spoke up enough to cover her silence as they laughed and fed Sophie bits of chicken from their own plates.

A scream caused Megan to whirl around.

"Help, please!" Susan Wilson stood under the gazebo, yelling and waving her arms.

The hem of her husband's pants was on fire. He was hopping around, swatting at the flames with his hands in a futile effort to put the fire out. He screamed in pain, his face torn with agony.

Jared didn't hesitate. Dishes went flying as he jerked the blanket out from beneath them, then raced toward the man. Like a bulldozer, Jared knocked Bill Wilson to the ground and wrapped the blanket around him. He held tight, snuffing out the flames. Bill lay very still for several seconds. Then he cried in pain, reaching down to hold on to his leg.

"Oh, thank you," Susan said.

Jared pulled back the blanket to inspect Bill's leg. "What happened?"

"Lighter fluid," Bill gasped and grimaced in pain. "It got on my pants when I was starting the briquettes. When I lit the match, it just ignited. It happened so fast, I didn't know what was going on. I didn't even realize." Bill spoke the words between gritted teeth.

Megan stood there helplessly, her two children pulling close against her legs for comfort.

Jared jerked his head toward her. "There's a first-aid kit in the back of my truck. Will you get it for me, please?"

With one nod, Megan turned and ran, calling over her shoulder to her children. "I'll be right back. Stay with Jared."

Her kids nodded solemnly. Little Caleb's face was crinkled, as though he might cry.

Megan pumped her legs hard and fast as she raced toward the parking lot. She found the first-aid kit with little trouble, then sprinted back to the gazebo. Poor Bill. He and Susan had just wanted to enjoy the evening as she and Jared had been doing.

Bill would be okay, though. And now that she thought of it, this interruption was good for her. It gave Megan an excuse to take her children home now. Before they got more involved with Jared Marshall.

She tried to ignore the buzzing inside her head. She was glad the incident hadn't escalated further, but seeing the flames flickering around Bill's pant leg had brought back another rush of memories. The emotions she'd experienced when the previous fire-control officer had informed her that Blaine was dead still clung to her like acrid wood smoke. A heavy lump formed in her throat. She couldn't get rid of her misgivings no matter how hard she tried. The experience felt fresh and new, as if it had happened today.

She'd told Jared she didn't want to get close to him. It was time to leave. Before her heart became even more entwined with this kind man she liked so much but refused to ever love.

Twenty minutes later, Jared had wrapped Frank's leg in a sterile bandage and a few plastic bags that he'd filled with ice he'd obtained from Susan's cooler chest. He loaded the Wilson family into their station wagon and waved goodbye. Susan sat in the driver's seat, planning to drive her husband to the hospital in Reno. There was no ambulance service in this small town. From what Jared could see, Bill's wounds were superficial. He'd been very lucky.

"You think he'll be all right?" Megan asked as she stood beside Jared and her children on the sidewalk.

The fading sunlight glimmered in the western sky, the air filled with the pungent aroma of cut grass.

Holding Caleb in his arms, Jared stared

at the taillights of the Wilson's car as they turned the corner and disappeared from view. "Yeah, he'll be okay. From what I could see, Bill received second-degree burns. The blisters will be painful, but they shouldn't do much damage to the muscle. He should heal fine."

Megan's forehead crinkled with worry, her eyes filled with empathy. Jared couldn't help wondering if she was thinking about her own husband and the pains he must have suffered when he'd been caught in the wildfire that took his life. A protective impulse flooded him with the desire to help, but he knew there was nothing he could do. They said time healed all wounds, but he had his doubts. Though he'd finally realized he wanted a romantic relationship with Megan, the pain from his past wasn't completely gone. He longed to push aside his own pain over his divorce and wished Megan could somehow get over losing her husband. He figured that was impossible, but he still hoped they both could find happiness again.

The puppy sat at their feet, silently panting. Even the little dog seemed to know this was not a happy occasion. A dark cloud of worry seemed to have blanketed them all.

Caleb reached out his hands and turned

Jared's face toward him. The boy's bottom lip was quivering. "What's gonna happen to Mr. Wilson?"

Jared exhaled a heavy sigh and met the child's eyes. Out of his peripheral vision, he saw little June clutching her mommy's hand as she leaned against the woman for support. The kids were scared, and he wanted to reassure them.

"Mr. Wilson is going to be okay," he said. "Have you ever had a burn on your hand or arm?"

June spoke in a thin, vague tone. "Yes, from Mommy's curling iron. It hurt really bad."

"That's right. But it healed up just fine, didn't it?"

The girl rubbed her hand and nodded, as if remembering the pain. "Yes, I can't even see the scar anymore."

"Well, Mr. Wilson might have scars, but his wounds should heal well, too. I think he's going to be all right."

June gave a little sigh of relief.

"When I grow up, I'm gonna be a wildfire fighter, too. I want to be a hero just like you and my dad," Caleb said with a determined lift of his head.

"Well, that's nice. It's a noble profession." Jared's smile widened. The boy's words gave him a sense of pride. It delighted him that Caleb considered his profession heroic. But then Jared glanced at Megan. She'd gone very still. Her breath stuttered to a halt. She stood apart from him, not meeting his eyes. Not moving, not breathing. As though she were suspended in time.

"It's time for us to go home, now." Megan's voice sounded low and firm. Disapproving.

"You sure? We didn't get to play Frisbee, yet," Jared said.

"I'm sorry, but I think it's best if we go, now." She reached out and pulled Caleb into her arms before setting him on his feet.

"Aww, can't we stay a little while longer?" the boy asked.

"It's getting late," she said.

"But we didn't get to play much with Sophie. I want to play Frisbee with Jared, too," June said.

The girl's words warmed Jared's heart. In the beginning, she hadn't liked him much, and he was relieved that her feelings had changed. And that's when Jared realized that, if he loved Megan, he'd also have to accept responsibility for her two children. He'd have to love them both like a father should. He wouldn't accept anything less. But if he ever broke up with Megan, it'd hurt more than he could bear. And Jared wasn't sure he wanted to take that chance. But if he didn't, he'd miss out on the joy a happy family life could bring to him. And he didn't want to forgo that experience. It was a difficult conundrum.

"Maybe another time," Megan said.

"Aww," Caleb groaned.

Megan ignored her complaining children and started packing up the scattered remnants of their picnic. Jared helped her, sensing she'd had enough. He still couldn't wrap his mind around what she'd told him. Because her husband had died in a wildfire, she'd written off ever loving another firefighter. He could understand her reticence. She didn't want to be hurt, just like him. But for some reason, her rejection bit him hard. Megan didn't want him, just as his ex-wife hadn't wanted him. He thought about trying to convince Megan that they should be together, but he wasn't sure he wanted to push her into something she didn't want.

He busied himself with folding up the ruined blanket. Megan packed the food items into the basket, and the kids bounded across the grass with the puppy in hot pursuit.

"You okay?" Jared asked Megan.

"Yes, I'm fine." But she didn't look at him. He laid a hand on her arm, longing to get through to her, yet wanting to run the other way. "We don't have to leave, you know. It's still early."

She stilled, finally meeting his eyes. "This isn't going to work, Jared."

He inwardly sighed, reading so much in those few words. But a desperate flush of despair rushed over him. He didn't want to lose her. He knew that now, deep in his heart. "I know you're worried about the kids. But I'd like to be a part of their lives. I'd like to be a part of your life, too, Megan."

He stepped near, remembering the night that he'd kissed her. There was hesitancy written in her eyes. She looked up, her expression sad and hopeful all at the same time. Her lips parted on a forlorn sigh.

"No. I can't, Jared. I've got to go." She brushed past him and reached to pick up the basket.

She tossed the refuse into the can and stood there for the count of three. Then, she turned. In her eyes, he saw all the sorrow of the world.

"I can't. Not again," she said.

He released a pent-up sigh and slid his hands into his pockets. "Megan, I'm not going to die anytime soon. If you're afraid of that, you can put it aside. Bill Wilson just had a little accident. It's not going to happen to me. I'm a good firefighter, and I don't usually have to work on the fire line anymore. I'm an administrator now. You can stop worrying about that. I wish you'd trust me."

She brushed her bangs back from her eyes. "Trust has nothing to do with it, Jared. You'll be up working in the fire camp and out on the line, to check on what's happening. I know how it works. As long as you're fighting fire, you'll be in harm's way. Blaine was good at his job, too. He didn't plan on dying either, but he did. You have no control over the winds or if the fire rolls over the top of you."

He felt a sinking despair. How could he fight against her fear? She didn't want him because he was a wildfire fighter. She was afraid. Of his dangerous profession. Of him. Afraid they might get close and then he'd get killed. Afraid it'd break her children's hearts. And maybe her heart, too.

"Any of us could die at any moment, Megan. It could happen anywhere, anytime, to any person. A house fire. A car accident. A brain aneurysm. Cancer. None of us knows the moment or hour when we could be hurt. But we can't live our lives in fear. I wish you'd have a little more faith in me. And maybe have a little faith in God, too."

She shook her head. "I can't take chances again. I don't have that luxury."

Gathering up the quilt, she turned and called to the children. "Come on, kids. We're going home."

Jared just stood there. His ex-wife had hated his profession. Not because it was dangerous, but because it required them to live in small, backward towns throughout the Western United States. A job he absolutely loved. Several times, Sharon had even been rude and condescending to his boss. She'd purposefully kept from passing on phone messages to him when his office had called. She'd done everything she could to get him to quit. But his work had sustained him through the painful divorce, and he'd vowed never again to allow a woman to jeopardize his career. But now, here he was again, facing another woman that didn't like his work, but for completely different reasons. And the result was the same.

Megan didn't want him, just as Sharon didn't want him.

"I'll take you home," he said, feeling lost and hurt all at the same time.

As they walked to his truck, got inside and

he drove them to his place so Megan could retrieve her vehicle, he couldn't help thinking that love wasn't worth this much hassle. It wasn't worth the pain. Maybe he was doomed to live his life alone. A single bachelor with no children of his own. No one to worry about. No one to love.

Unless he could convince Megan differently.

Chapter Twelve

Boom! Kaboom!

Megan jerked awake, her eyes staring wide at the ceiling in her bedroom. Faint sunlight filtered through the lacy curtains. She glanced at the digital clock sitting on the nightstand. Six o'clock in the morning. Sunrise. She groaned and rolled over onto her side. Maybe she could get a few more minutes of sleep.

"Mommy! Mommy!" Caleb and June scurried into the room together.

The two kids jumped smack in the middle of the bed and burrowed against Megan's sides.

"Hi, sweethearts." She kissed each one on the forehead and wrapped her arms around them.

Boom!

Caleb gasped and ducked his head beneath the covers. "The whole world is blowing up."

His muffled words made Megan chuckle. "No, sweetie. It's just the cannon blast telling us that it's Founder's Day and we should get up and go to the parade."

"Is that why we're not opening the restaurant until later?" June asked.

"Yep. We have the morning off. It was kind of nice to sleep in for a change, wasn't it?" She tickled them both, enjoying their squeals of laughter.

"What time is the parade?" June asked.

"Ten o'clock, but we'll need to arrive early if we want to get a good place to set up our lawn chairs. Shall we get ready and go?" she asked.

"Yeah." Caleb nodded solemnly.

"Definitely," June said.

They scrambled off the bed and raced into their rooms to get dressed. Megan was glad they had this opportunity to feel like a normal family. The parade would fortify them for the hectic workday ahead at the restaurant. No doubt they'd be swamped by lots of customers.

Two hours later, Megan had made the kids breakfast burritos and driven them over to Main Street. She parked the truck in the alleyway behind the bakery, then let them help her haul their chairs up the sidewalk. The sun blazed bright, the wind wafting the smell of popcorn from a vending booth where the cheerleader squad from the high school was trying to make a little extra money for their team. The steady flow of people told Megan it would be a large crowd, even for a small town like Minoa.

Parents laughed with their children, some carrying balloons and tall glasses of lemonade from another vendor—the baseball team, trying to earn enough money to buy new uniforms. Megan purchased a drink for her and the kids to share, glad to contribute to the cause. Blaine had played baseball in high school, and she couldn't help feeling a bit nostalgic today. The last time she'd come to this parade, he'd been by her side, carrying Caleb on his broad shoulders.

"Where's Jared?" June asked.

"I have no idea," Megan replied, wishing her children would forget about the man.

"Can we sit with him?" Caleb said.

"I don't know if we can even find him in this crowd." Megan spoke reluctantly. She hadn't planned on sitting with Jared to watch the parade and would rather avoid him, if possible. Being near him was wreaking havoc on her nerves. Mostly because she liked him so much.

A man bumped into her, propelling her toward another woman standing in front of her. Megan caught herself just in time, barely avoiding a collision.

"Excuse me, ma'am," the man said.

She smiled with understanding. The crush of people was heavy this year, which meant the restaurant would be very busy this afternoon. In years past, Megan had always gauged the customers they had at the restaurant off of the crowd attending the parade. It looked as if they'd have plenty of business.

"Hi, Megan." Susan Wilson waved at her from the street corner.

A woman with long, dark hair and a cheery face, Susan sat with her children on a blanket spread across the small bit of grass in front of the hardware store. Her husband sat in a wicker chair beside her.

Megan paused to say hello. "Hi, there. How are you doing, Bill?"

The burly man smiled from beneath the wide brim of his straw hat and carefully stretched his legs out in front of him. He wore knee-length shorts, exposing his left calf wrapped in a white bandage. A pair of crutches rested on the ground at his feet.

"I'm good, thanks to you and Jared. I don't know what I would have done if you hadn't been there in the park that day."

A sudden warmth flooded her cheeks. "I didn't do anything. It was all Jared's quick thinking."

"Well, we're beyond grateful."

"We sure are," Susan said. "And it was kind of you to bring dinner in the next day. I've never been so happy to see my Bill tackled to the ground. If Jared hadn't done that, Bill might have gone up in flames."

Megan doubted it, but the damage to Bill's leg could have been much worse. The entire incident could have been catastrophic. Thank goodness Jared had been there. She knew the world needed firefighters. Especially ones as skilled and caring as him.

But when she thought back on Caleb telling Jared he wanted to be a wildfire fighter when he grew up, Megan's blood went cold and her heart turned to ice. The thought of losing her dear little child to a fire like the one that had killed his father made her tremble with fear. She hated to hurt Jared's feelings by telling him she didn't want to date him anymore, but she couldn't take the chance that she'd love and lose him, either.

"I'm just glad you're going to be all right." She patted Bill's shoulder.

"Megan! Over here."

Megan lifted her arm to shield her eyes against the sun. Connie sat with Tim in front of the Forest Service office. She was waving to get Megan's attention. A number of fire personnel sat clustered around her, all of them laughing and chatting.

"Come on." Taking Caleb's hand, she led her children over to them.

"Hi, Megan," Tessa greeted her, sitting on a bench beside Sean.

"Hi, buddy." Zach swooped Caleb up in his arms and whirled the boy around. Caleb's laughter filled the air.

"Do me, too," June said. She reached her arms out and Zach obliged her.

With her children occupied by the strong firefighter, Megan folded out her lawn chairs and set them close beside Connie and Gayle beneath the wide spread of an elm tree.

"Hi there," Connie smiled.

"Hello. Looks like we haven't missed anything."

"No, the parade hasn't started yet."

"I feared we wouldn't be able to find a decent spot. It's crowded this year," Megan said.

"You always have a place here with us," Gayle said.

Megan returned the woman's smile. She chatted for a few moments with several other hotshot employees. They all greeted her with friendly smiles. "Where's Jared?" Gayle asked.

Megan stared at the woman, startled by her question. "How should I know?"

"I thought you two were together, now."

Several people were staring at her, and Megan's face heated up like road flares. She wanted to dispel any illusions that she and Jared were romantically involved but figured it would come out wrong. "No, we're just friends."

Okay, it sounded lame, but she said it anyway. *Friends* was nice and neutral. Wasn't it?

"Sure, uh-huh. Anyone can see that you light up like a fire engine every time he's around. And he obviously feels the same about you," Gayle teased, throwing a knowing look in her direction.

Megan stammered and blinked, feeling odd and anxious. Two months ago, she could hardly imagine being in a serious relationship with any man except Blaine. And this situation made her reevaluate what Jared meant to her. He was just a nice man who had been kind to her and her children. There wasn't anything else to it.

Or was there?

No! There couldn't be. She couldn't allow it. But she didn't respond to Susan. Any protests would only draw more attention to the topic. Better to just remain quiet.

"It's starting, it's starting." June jumped up and down and clapped her little hands.

Music sounded as horses from the equine club clattered past on the street. The two lead riders carried the US and state flags.

Tim immediately stood, removed his hat and placed his right hand over his heart as he showed respect for his country. Little Caleb copied the man's actions exactly, looking so much like his father that it made Megan's eyes sting. She blinked, feeling grateful and worried at the same time. Her children needed a father. No wonder they'd become so attached to Jared.

"I can't see." Caleb craned his neck this way and that, trying to look around the hefty woman standing in front of him.

"Well, we can't have that." Zach lifted the boy up onto his wide shoulders.

"Yay! I can see everything now." Caleb laughed.

Megan sat in her chair and pulled June

onto her lap. The girl leaned back with a sigh of contentment, enjoying the view. Megan breathed deeply of June's fruity shampoo. It felt good to sit down and enjoy the parade.

The hotshot crew's pumper trucks drove by. Several hotshots wearing yellow Nomex shirts stood in the back. And standing in the middle was Smokey the Bear, tossing candy into the street.

"Look, Mom! It's Smokey the Bear," June cried, her eyes wide with awe.

"And Jared!" Caleb said.

Sure enough, Jared stood beside Smokey, tossing candy to the children.

"Hey, Smokey," Caleb yelled and waved his arms over his head to get the bear's attention.

The bear waved back. With the mob of people, it was difficult to tell where he was looking, but Megan saw Jared point toward them. She had no doubt that Smokey was responding to her children.

"Come on, let's get some candy." Zach ran to the street curb with the kids to pick up a few pieces.

Connie leaned closer to Megan. "They asked Jared to play the part of Smokey this year, but he said no."

Confusion filled Megan's mind as she glanced at the woman. "Really?"

Connie nodded and pointed at the bear. "Yes, he told Tim that he didn't want to usurp Caleb's and June's memory of their father."

Megan froze. Once again, Jared's thoughtfulness touched her deeply. She didn't know what to think about this revelation. Seeing how much Jared cared for her kids did something to her inside.

At that precise moment, Smokey lifted a fistful of candy and launched it straight at June's and Caleb's feet. The children crowed with laughter as they happily picked up every piece.

Then both Jared and Smokey waved, their heads turned toward her. And heaven help her, she couldn't keep from lifting her hand in the air to wave back.

The pumper truck passed on by, and then came the high school marching band. The trumpets and bass drums pounded in Megan's chest.

"So, how's it going with Jared?" Connie asked in a low voice for her ears alone.

"What do you mean?" Megan said.

"You know. With the catering gig."

Oh. Funny how Megan thought she meant romantically. "Fine."

Connie sat back in her chair.

"And how about between the two of you?" Connie pressed.

Okay, here it was. The heart of the issue. But Megan decided to play it cool. "Fine. Like I've been saying all along, we're just friends."

"Has he asked you out again?"

Megan didn't look at her. She didn't want to tell the waitress about their date in the park. "You know we can't be anything more than friends. I'm never falling for another firefighter."

Connie snorted. "That's a bunch of phooey. Jared's a great catch. You should make an exception."

Megan didn't respond. She was not going to get sucked into another discussion about this. Why wouldn't people just leave her alone about it?

Connie leaned forward and met her eyes. "And what if you avoid him and it ends up being a big regret in your life?"

Megan froze. That thought had never entered her mind. She'd been so worried about being hurt again that she hadn't considered the possible regrets. But the thought of never seeing Jared again left her cold and hollow inside.

Her heart told her to just sit back, relax and enjoy the blessings life brought her way.

But her memories sent a warning chill up her spine. Life wasn't easy and it hadn't always been good to her. If she wasn't careful, she was going to fall head over heels in love with Jared Marshall, and then there'd be no turning back.

Immediately following the parade, Megan and the kids made their way over to the restaurant. Frank was already there, setting up the salad bar and firing up the grill. And within twenty minutes, the place was crammed to capacity. A dull roar filled the space, with people laughing and talking all at once.

Megan was helping Connie wait on tables when Jared walked in. Caleb and June sat at the front counter, munching on ham sandwiches and fries. As Jared joined them there, Megan stayed busy doing other things.

"Can you wait on Jared?" she whispered to Connie as she shuttled a tray of drinks over to the farthest booth in the diner.

Connie shook her head, speaking low. "No can do. My boss said she'd take the counter and refill drinks today. I've got the tables and dining room."

Megan almost groaned at the reminder.

"You know, I am your boss. I'm allowed to change my mind."

Connie just laughed and hurried past, balancing four plates of food. "You definitely are my boss, but I didn't think you were a coward."

Hmm. Megan would love to fire Connie right now, but knew it'd do no good. She loved the snippy waitress dearly, and she definitely wasn't a coward.

Or was she? Where Jared was concerned, Megan wasn't sure anymore.

No matter, Connie obviously wasn't going to wait on the man, so Megan would have to do it whether she liked it or not. "Hi, Jared. What'll you have?" she asked in a crisp, businesslike tone as she slid a stack of menus into their holder.

He flashed that amazing smile and jerked his head toward the kids. "I'll have what they're having. And a diet cola."

He brushed his fingertips against Megan's arm. A soft, gentle caress that sent a zing of awareness racing down her spine. His eyes sparkled like sapphires. A dimple showed in his left cheek and she caught a whiff of his spicy aftershave.

"One ham and cheese with fries, coming up." She quickly wrote the order down and snapped it up for Frank.

"Wow, you're busy today, huh?" Jared asked.

"Yep, we are. One of the busiest days of the year."

"Did you enjoy the parade?"

She nodded. "Of course."

"I saw you and waved."

A cold part of her heart went all warm and mushy inside. She couldn't deny his smile. "Yes, I understand that you didn't want to be Smokey this year."

She spoke low, so no one would overhear her. The identity of Smokey the Bear was usually kept a secret from the kids.

"No, I didn't think it'd be right… Who told you that?" he asked.

"Connie." Her voice wobbled, betraying her nervousness.

"I hope I didn't hurt your feelings by being in the parade. But as the FMO, I'm kind of expected to ride along…"

She held up a hand, cutting him off. "No, it's okay. Really. I'm fine."

He released a giant exhale of relief. "It looked like Caleb and June were having fun."

"Of course. They love the parade every year."

Scooping ice into a glass, Megan filled Jared's drink and slid it onto the counter with a straw, then bustled on to the next customer.

Giving him no more than a nod. Giving him no more time to chat.

Ten minutes later, she set his plate of food in front of him. The kids finished their meals and went into the back office to watch some TV. Even they didn't want to be out in the crazy chaos of the restaurant today. Megan glanced over at Jared's seat, but he wasn't there. Just a crisp twenty-dollar bill tucked beneath his plate.

Good. He must have gotten tired of her ignoring him and left. That's what she needed him to do. And yet, she felt an inkling of remorse. When he wasn't around, she actually missed him. And that insight stunned her.

A moment later, she got another good shock. She looked up and saw Jared balancing a gray tub as he cleared a vacant table. Pete Rawlins and Dave Winton, both squad bosses on the hotshot crew, sat nearby heckling him.

"Hey, boss, I didn't know you were a dishwasher as well as an FMO." Pete grinned.

"Yeah, you clear dishes away real well. Is this a new side job you've taken on?" Dave asked.

Jared didn't stop working as he showed a good-natured smile. "I'm just helping out a friend. I'm multitalented, boys. Laugh it up.

I'll be sure to think of something fun for you two to do on the next wildfire."

Though spoken with a laugh, his words held a veiled threat. Megan didn't think he'd do anything mean, but he got Pete's and Dave's attention. The two men ducked their heads over their double cheeseburgers and didn't say another word.

Ignoring the din of noise, Megan walked over and touched Jared's arm. "Thanks for the help, but you don't need to do this. I'll get to it soon."

He tossed her a friendly smile and shrugged. "I don't mind. I don't have anything better to do. Besides, I've never seen you this busy before. It's a good thing you hired extra waitresses, but even with that, I think you need the help today."

Yes, she did, but this wasn't his job.

"Really, don't do that. We can manage without you." She tried to take the dishcloth away from him, but he moved it out of her reach.

"It's okay. Really," he said.

With a few quick wipes of the clean table, he nodded and carried the tub to the back washroom.

Thinking that was settled and he'd move on now, she hurried about the diner, meeting everyone's needs. Too busy to spend any more time worrying about Jared and his generosity. But she couldn't seem to get him off her mind. And she admitted only to herself that she wished things could be different between them. Much, much different.

Chapter Thirteen

Megan locked the front door behind the last customer of the evening. Finally, it was closing time. Finally, she could go home and soak her aching feet.

From the wide windows fronting the restaurant, she saw that bright stars glittered in the night sky, the tall lights outside adding a yellow glow to the street below. Slinging his jacket over his shoulder, Frank walked out into the dining room, his car keys dangling from his fingers. In his other hand, he held a pack of gum. He'd quit smoking five weeks earlier and had started chewing gum furiously to help alleviate his cravings. Megan was proud of his accomplishment and continued to encourage him not to give up the fight. So far, it was working.

Connie stood beside him, her short curly

hair looking wilted by steam from the dishwashers in the back room. They'd both worked hard today, and Megan loved them for it. They were good friends as well as employees.

"Thank you so much for all your help today. You guys are the absolute best," Megan said.

Frank's face flushed red with pleasure. "Anytime."

"You're welcome. Will you be okay if we head out now?" Connie asked.

"Yes, I'm just going to finish up a few things and go home," Megan said.

Connie shook a large foam cup that jingled pleasantly with coins. A wad of green bills stuck up over the top. "Lots of good tips today."

Yes, they'd been crazy busy, but the business was good. Megan smiled and let them out the front door before locking it again behind them. Shoving the key into the pocket of her apron, she turned to assess the order of the diner. Connie hadn't failed her. Everything looked in great shape for the next day's breakfast shift, except the floors that needed to be mopped. But that would have to wait until tomorrow. Nothing left to do tonight except total the receipts, then turn off the lights and go home.

Walking to the back office, she glanced in at her two children, sleeping together on the little cot she'd set up for them. She gazed at their serene faces, so sweet in the dim light. Another thirty minutes of counting out the receipts, then she could gather them up and take them home. Tomorrow was Sunday. A day off work for her.

Thank goodness.

A slight noise caught her attention. She tilted her head to listen. A whooshing sound came from the kitchen. Maybe Frank or Connie had left the water running.

She stepped over to the doorway and peered around the corner. Jared stood in front of the sink, mopping the linoleum floors. He twirled the heavy mop around an area, then dipped it into the sudsy water of the bucket and sloshed the mop up and down to rinse it out.

For several moments, she watched him work, stunned that he'd stayed until closing time. She'd been so busy that she'd almost forgotten about him. She thought he'd left hours ago. But no. He'd obviously been washing dishes all afternoon and evening. He'd worked as hard as her staff, and she was grateful.

"I thought you had left," she said, leaning against the doorjamb.

He jerked and snapped his head around, almost losing his grip on the mop stick.

"Hey! You startled me." He flashed her a smile so bright that it brought a hard lump to her throat.

She jutted her chin toward the bucket. "You don't need to do that. You've already done too much. Thanks for all your help today. I already owe you so much."

Oh, maybe she shouldn't have said that. If he asked her out on another date, she'd have to say no and she didn't want to hurt him again.

"It's no problem." He lifted the stringy mop into the wringer and pressed hard on the lever. Water gushed through the holes on the wringer plate.

"Really, I can finish up," she said.

He barely glanced her way. "It's okay. I've got this. If you'll give me just a few more minutes, you can get the kids up and I'll walk you out to your truck so you can go home. I want to make sure you're safe before I leave you."

His consideration touched her heart. It'd been a long time since a man had looked after her, and it felt good. Too good.

"You mean your truck, don't you?"

"Hmm?" He released the lever and slapped the mop back onto the floor before swirling it around another section.

"The truck belongs to you," she reminded him.

"Oh, yeah. That." He waved his hand, as if the truck was no big deal.

Great. He just kept making it more difficult not to like him. If he wasn't so handsome and nice, she could find a way to get angry at him. But as it stood, she couldn't very well dislike a man who was always bailing her out of trouble. Could she?

She folded her arms, admiring the way his back muscles flexed and moved as he swirled the mop around on the floor. His strong hands held the heavy mop stick effortlessly, as though it weighed nothing at all.

"Where'd you learn to mop like that?" she asked.

With the toe of his boot, he propelled the bucket past her and out into the dining room. With swift, short movements, he kept working while he talked. "From my mom. My dad died when I was about June's age. It was tough on the family, but my mom was strong, just like you. She worked hard and kept us together, the way you're doing for your kids."

"Oh." Megan looked away, feeling more confused than ever. Somehow knowing this bit of personal information about Jared only showed how much they had in common. If anyone understood what her kids were going through by losing their father, Jared did.

Trying to ignore him, she opened the cash register and sat in a corner booth to count up the receipts. If he wanted to help her, she wouldn't argue. Her lower back ached and she was too tired to care. She just didn't have the strength to fight him tonight.

He mopped his way around the room, reaching far beneath each table to clean the floors. And after all the customers they'd had that day, the floors needed it.

Finally, he circled back around to her. Clutching the receipts in her hand, she slid out of the booth as he drew near enough to touch her. He stuck the mop into the bucket for a final rinse, then stood there, strong, safe and dependable. The kind of man she could rely on to look after her kids. And her heart. But that had no bearing on the turmoil rumbling around inside of her mind. God would determine their futures. Neither she nor Jared had a say as to whether or not he was killed in a wildfire. And she hated feeling vulnerable. Hated being afraid.

She looked up into his eyes, feeling mesmerized and frozen in place. She couldn't move. Could barely breathe.

"Megan, trust me. Just trust me. I'll never do you wrong. I promise." He whispered the words, his lips curving into a slow, melting smile.

He leaned his head down and kissed her. Gently. A soft caress she readily embraced. He tasted of peppermint, and she lifted her free hand to place her palm against his chest, just over his heart. Her fingers tightened in the folds of his shirt, the solid wall of muscles warm and vibrant beneath her touch. She longed to confide in him. To tell him all the doubts rumbling around inside her heart. To cast her fears aside and rely on him forever more.

She burrowed nearer, feeling the solid beat of his heart beneath her fingertips. She shifted her weight, returning his kiss. Breathing him in.

"Jared, I just— I've already lost one husband. I can't lose another one. I've got two kids to think about. We can't do this."

"Yes, we can," he whispered against her lips. "We've both been afraid for a long time now. Afraid of commitment. Afraid of being hurt again. But I think it's time for us to trust again. To believe in the Lord and in each other. It's going to be okay. I promise you that. I want to see more of you and the kids. Just say you'll give me a chance. Please."

She melted against him, her lips pliant beneath his as he kissed her again. She wanted to believe him. She really did. But what about the future? What if…?

"Mommy?"

She broke away and inhaled a trembling breath.

Caleb walked into the dining room, rubbing his sleepy eyes.

"I'm right here, son." Her voice sounded shaky to her ears.

"Can we go home now?" the boy asked as she lifted him into her arms. He wrapped his legs around her waist as she cuddled him close against her neck.

"Yes, sweetie. We're going right now."

She glanced nervously at Jared, hoping her son hadn't seen her in Jared's embrace. She wouldn't know how to explain it. Not when she didn't understand it herself. She mustn't forget that all good things came to an end. Just like the fairy tale Cinderella, the elegant coach turned back into a pumpkin at midnight. Megan had to go back to her ordinary, safe life. Without Jared, or any other man that might leave her with another broken heart.

Jared wheeled the mop bucket into the back and dumped the dirty water. When he returned to the dining room, Megan had shut off all but the night-light and had June and Caleb waiting to walk out to the parking lot.

She locked the front door and Jared escorted them to their truck. She breathed in great drafts of cool night air that smelled of honeysuckle and rain. Jared waited until they were safely inside the vehicle and buckled into their seats, then he leaned against Megan's door.

"I'll give you a call tomorrow," he said.

She blinked. "No, please don't."

"Why not?"

She looked away. "You know why."

Frankly, she was lonely. And he was steady, kind, good-looking and fun to be with. It didn't help that her son adored him, too. But working with this man and loving him were two different things.

He reached out and lifted her chin, forcing her to meet his eyes. "That's not going to stop me, Meg. I can't fight my feelings anymore. I know you feel it, too. There's no use denying it. You know that now, don't you?"

She nodded, still feeling the throb of his

kiss against her lips. She'd never met a man so determined, so focused on what he wanted. And it pleased, yet dismayed, her to know that she was his target. That he wanted her and her children. To be a family with her.

"Tomorrow won't change anything, Jared. Please, if you really care for me, let me go." She rolled up the window and started up the truck. He stepped back as she pulled away. And she didn't look back, no matter how badly she wanted to.

Jared waited for Megan to pull out of the parking lot. Then, he drove home to his lonely house. He thought about the things Megan had told him and wondered if it was worth pursuing her any longer. After what he'd gone through with Sharon, he wanted to be angry at Megan for continuing to push him away. But he couldn't. She'd suffered enough already. Instead of anger, he wanted to comfort her. To take her into his arms and love and protect her. But he figured that was the last thing she wanted from him.

He pulled into his driveway and killed the engine. The porch light was on and the chirp of crickets escorted him as he headed up the sidewalk. In the gloomy night shadows, he unlocked the door to his house and went inside. In the kitchen, he'd left one light on, for the dog. Sophie galloped toward him, her puppy ears flopping. She yipped and wriggled a greeting against the dog gate where he'd blocked her off so she would have enough room to move but couldn't soil the carpets. He stepped over the barricade and she jumped at his feet. He reached down to pet her and she peed in excitement.

He laughed. "Yes, I'm glad to see you, too."

First, he scooped her up and took her out onto the back lawn, then praised her when she pottied in the right place.

"Good girl. Oh, yes, you're such a sweet girl. A wonderful little dog." He rubbed her soft fur and cuddled her before taking her back inside.

He checked to make sure she still had plenty of food and water. He didn't mind that she'd had one accident on the floor. After all, it wasn't her fault. Because he'd spent all day helping Megan at the restaurant, he'd been gone longer than he'd planned. Without a word, he cleaned up the mess, then took Sophie with him to bed. She curled into a ball beside him, and he lay there, thinking.

Megan didn't want him to pursue her. She was afraid he might get killed fighting a wildfire. He understood that. But he was determined to show her that life together was better than not being together at all. They couldn't live their lives in constant fear, because no matter what, bad things happened to good people. And one day, hopefully when they were both very old, they would pass on. But they had to enjoy their blessings while they still could.

He'd been lonely for so long. So hurt and fearful of loving someone else. But he no longer felt that way. Megan and her two little kids had wormed their way into his heart, and he wanted to build a family with them. To be a loving husband and a father to her two sweet children. To build a future and grow old together, sharing a full and rich life.

Suddenly everything became crystal clear, and that's when he realized he loved Megan, June and Caleb Rocklin. His love for them had come upon him slowly, softly. Something he'd never sought out or expected. But it was there just the same. He loved them. More than anything else in the world. And his feelings gave him the courage to take a second chance at love.

It seemed so simple when he thought of it that way. So amazing and wonderful. The future stood before them, filled with magnificent possibilities. And all he had to do was convince Megan that they should be together. In spite of what he did for a living. In spite of her misgivings.

Easier said than done.

In the darkness, Jared closed his eyes and prayed. For the first time in a long time, he asked for God's help. To help him woo Megan. To somehow ease her doubts and fears. Because Jared was not turning his back on her, no matter what. He'd wait forever, if that's what it took. But his heart was completely and utterly tied to hers now. Failure was not an option. Not with her. Not for him. Not ever again. Because he was finally ready to fight for her love.

Chapter Fourteen

On Wednesday, they got another wildfire. Like before, Jared woke Megan in the middle of the night, giving her as much notice as possible. Hearing his deep voice brought her instantly awake. She grabbed for the notepad and pen she kept on the bedside table and took down the pertinent information. When she had everything, she said goodbye, then called her people to put them on alert.

Two hours later, Megan had dropped her two groggy kids off at her child-care provider's house and headed up onto the mountain just as the sun was breaking across the eastern sky. Since this was the first day of the fire and they'd have to set up the dining tent, there was no way Megan was going to bring her kids along. No sirree. She wanted them safely in town, where no harm could befall them.

A group of firefighters helped Megan's crew set up the tent, and it went together without any problems. As they unloaded supplies from the back of her truck, Megan paused and dusted off her hands, wondering where Jared was. Usually, he was here to greet her. And she admitted only to herself that she missed him.

Trying to avoid her own wayward thoughts, she went back to work. She was restocking the industrial-sized refrigerator with gallon-sized Cubitainers when she felt a hand touch her shoulder. She turned in surprise.

"Jared!"

"Hi there," he said, his mouth curved in a half smile. "You doing okay?"

"Sure." She nodded, feeling odd and fumbly in his presence. And yet, a buzzing awareness thrummed through her veins. She couldn't deny the happy bubble that rose in her chest, and she realized how much this man had come to mean to her and her family. She'd fought her growing attraction for so long. And right there, she had the insane notion that maybe she was wrong about Jared. That maybe, if she didn't gather her courage and take a second chance on love, she would never experience the joy, either. And she'd have to live with that regret for the rest of her life.

"Sorry I couldn't be here when you arrived," he said. "Were there any mishaps in putting up the tent this time?"

"Nope, everything went just like clockwork."

He glanced around, looking eager. "Did you bring the kids with you this time?"

"No, they're in town."

"Is there anything I can do?" His gaze brushed past her to the cartons of milk she was stacking neatly inside the fridge. His consideration touched her heart. She felt as though he genuinely cared and wanted to help.

"No, we've about got it taken care of. I'm just getting ready to head back," she said, trying to keep her wobbly voice calm and even.

He took a step closer, and she stared at his wide chest, where his brass Forest Service badge gleamed against his left shirt pocket.

"Have you thought any more about what I said?" he asked.

She didn't pretend to not understand. "No, my answer hasn't changed."

She glanced up into his eyes in time to see the hurt there.

"Megan, please don't push me away."

His voice sounded low and calm. Drawing her in. Convincing her to change her mind. But she caught herself just in time.

"No, Jared. I've got work to do."

She turned away, shutting off his next comment. She'd stacked another row of Cubitainers into the refrigerator before she turned around, expecting to see him still there. But he was gone. She'd never felt more lonely in her life.

Three days later, Jared stood near the fire line, supervising the unloading of three giant crawler tractors. Their steel treads would cleat the earth, giving them the traction and power to push tons of dirt, trees and anything else out of their paths as the crews built a fire line.

Jared tried to focus on his work. Three miserable days had passed in which he'd forced himself to stay away from Megan. To give her some space. He wasn't ready to give up on her, but he figured she needed time to think. To decide what it was she really wanted in life. And hopefully to realize that she missed him, too. But it hadn't been easy. One of his men had radioed him an hour earlier to say that she'd arrived in the fire camp and was unloading food supplies. She had the kids with her today, but Jared had resisted the urge to go and see them all. Maybe tomorrow.

Heavy smoke filled the air, the sky a red, angry glow caused by the fire. Dale Carter, the equipment manager, stood nearby, talking on his radio. He pressed a finger to his ear, trying to hear over the rumbling noise of engines.

"What's that you say?" Dale yelled.

Jared barely glanced the man's way as he waved his arms to indicate to the driver where the first tractor should begin digging a wide trench of fire line. A few moments later, Jared felt a tap on his shoulder. He whirled around and pushed back his hard hat.

"We may have to move this equipment back down to the fire camp," Dale yelled above the growling roar.

"Why is that?" Jared asked.

"The fire has burned across the road about four miles below the camp. It's closed off the road and shut off our access. Some squirrelly winds are whipping the fire around. There wasn't any notice. The Minoa Hotshots are already there, trying to stop it. A couple of them are trapped in a chimney area."

Jared froze. His entire body went cold with dread. "Which men?"

"Sean Nash and Zach Carpenter. Sean's the

one that gave us the warning. He alerted his crew to the danger and got them out in time, but he and Zach are still in there. Word has it that they're trapped by flames. Helitack is trying to figure out a way to fly in and evacuate them, but there's nowhere to land safely."

A sick feeling settled in the pit of Jared's stomach. Sean's and Zach's lives were in danger. But something else bothered Jared. Something closer to home.

Megan was in the camp, but she wouldn't be here long. A quick in-and-out, just to drop off food supplies. She'd be leaving for town soon and might be trapped on her way down the mountain. Unless he could catch her first.

"I've got to go warn the caterer. She might be caught on that road unaware." With a wave of his hand, Jared tore off toward his truck.

His blood rushed through his veins with urgency. One thought pounded his brain. Megan and the kids. He had to get to them. Had to warn them. Had to keep them safe.

He drove at a fast clip along the dirt road, a stream of dust rising from his tires to mark his passing. Urgency built within him. A fear that he wouldn't arrive in time. He must warn them. He had to reach them in time.

Five minutes later, he pulled into the fire camp. He parked his truck near the mobile kitchen and hopped out. It was three in the afternoon, but it didn't matter. It felt more like nightfall. The sky was filled with gray smoke and a red haze just beyond. A mixture of dawn and twilight. Unique, beautiful and eerie.

Rows of men and a few women stood lined up for a meal, their faces black with soot. The kitchen never closed its doors. Hand crews came off the fire line at all hours of the day, always ravenous and thirsty. They ate whenever they got the chance.

"Hi, Jared." Frank waved to him from the serving window as he spooned heaping mounds of mashed potatoes, gravy and cube steak onto empty tin plates.

"Where's Megan?" Jared called impatiently.

Frank pointed toward the road, a cheerful smile on his ruddy face. "You just missed her. She left about five minutes ago."

A flush of panic rushed over Jared. He could try calling her cell phone, but knew she wouldn't have reception at this high, remote elevation. And even if she did, she was bumping along the dirt road and wouldn't hear her phone ring.

Without another word, he raced back to his truck, turned the key, popped the vehicle into gear and tore off down the road. Frantic with worry. Desperate to hurry. Megan and the kids could get caught in the fire.

He had to find them. Had to stop them from going any farther. To bring them back to the camp where they'd be safe. He'd promised Megan that he'd protect her. That this catering job would never endanger her or the kids. Then June had almost been badly injured by the dining tent. And now this. Jared had asked Megan to trust him. He'd told her that he'd watch out for her. That he had her back. And now, he might be too late.

Chapter Fifteen

"The old gray mare, she ain't what she used to be. Many long years ago." Megan sang the words to the funny song, smiling at her children's laughter.

"Sing it again, Mom," Caleb said.

Sitting in the back, he was buckled into his booster seat with June right beside him. A trail of dust sifted into the air behind them on the dirt road. Within an hour, they'd be back in town. Then Megan would take a quick inventory of her shelves so the afternoon delivery truck could replenish her food supplies. She'd make a quick stop at the restaurant, to ensure things were running smoothly there. And after that, she would take her kids to their house for a home-cooked meal.

They were doing just fine. For the first time in a long time, she'd paid off some nagging bills and was in the black financially. And all because of her catering work on the fire lines. She owed Jared a debt of gratitude.

"Only if you'll sing it with me this time," Megan said, feeling happy and relieved.

They'd just dropped off the groceries for the fire camp and were on their way home. Even with the heavy workload, they'd had a fun day together. The only thing missing was Jared. And Megan was beginning to rethink her promise to stay away from the man. Because in all honesty, she missed him. Badly.

"I'll sing," June said.

The girl broke into song, her voice high and sweet. But Megan didn't join in. She was lost in thoughts about Jared and their relationship. But when she focused on the road ahead, she gasped.

"What's the matter, Mommy?" June asked.

Megan stared in front of her, stunned by what she saw. Fire had come up through the canyon and popped over the ridge. It was burning across the road. A flickering dance of five-foot flames arched toward them. Inaccessible. She couldn't understand it. How had this happened? Where had the fire come from? The road had been perfectly clear an hour earlier. They had to go back the way they'd come, to seek safety in the fire camp. Right now.

She tapped the brake and slowed the truck. "We've got to turn around."

The kids stared out the window, their mouths and eyes round with surprise. They stared at the red flames flickering in the bushes. The wind was driving it straight toward them.

"Mommy?" Caleb said, his voice high and nervous.

"It's okay, kids. We're gonna be okay." Even as she said the words, Megan hoped it was true.

June started to cry.

"It'll be all right, sweetheart. We'll just go back the way we came. The fire camp isn't far away. They've got lots of strong firefighters and big fire hoses there. They'll keep us safe. No problem." In spite of her words, sheer panic coursed through her veins. The desperation to keep her children safe.

"But why is the fire over here, Mom?" Caleb asked in his matter-of-fact voice.

"I don't know, honey. Maybe it got out of control. There's lots of reasons. But I want to get out of here right now. We can find out the details later on." She tried to sound reasonable. To keep her children calm. But all she could think about was the fire that had killed Blaine. She'd been told that it had happened so fast. Without explanation. Without any notice. And he'd died as a result.

She spun the steering wheel, urgent to turn the truck around. It was tight on the narrow road. Not enough room. The wheels bounced over clumps of sage and rabbit brush. The kids' heads bobbed as the tires dipped into a low rut.

Thump!

The truck jerked hard. Megan pressed on the gas, but the tires whirred without going anywhere.

"What's wrong?" June asked, her voice trembling with distress.

"We've hit something. Stay here while I check it out," Megan said.

She opened her door and hopped out. Thick, pungent wood smoke filled her lungs, making her cough. Even from this distance, she felt the heat of the fire like the blast from a furnace and pushed her legs to hurry faster.

"No, Mommy! Stay here with us," June cried from the open truck door.

"I'm just checking the tires," Megan yelled back.

She rounded the vehicle, looking at the wheels. When she saw the problem, her heart sank. She'd hit a wide tree stump, the left rear tire high ended and unable to move. She pushed against the fender with all her might, but it wouldn't budge. She couldn't get it free. Not without some serious help.

She knew she had a tire jack with the spare in back. Glancing at the blazing fire, she realized there wasn't enough time for that. They had to get out of here. Right now.

She coughed, the acrid smoke choking her lungs and burning her eyes. Above the dull crackling roar, she heard her children crying. The greedy flames were moving closer. So near to them now. Moving fast. Tracking them. The only way to safety was back to the camp. But she knew she couldn't race the fire. She would never be able to run fast enough to outpace the flames. Certainly not with two little kids in tow.

Think! Where could she go? What could she do?

Another sound caught her attention, just to the south of her. Gosser's Creek. It was close by. Blaine had taken her fishing there a couple of times over the past years. In some places, it was quite wide, the cool, clear water rushing past. If she could get the kids down there, they could take shelter in the creek. It wasn't foolproof. Many firefighters lost their lives even when they took sanctuary in a creek bed. But it was their only chance.

Jared drove like a lunatic. Much too fast on this rutted road. But he didn't care about the shocks on his truck. They could be repaired. Megan and the kids were the most important thing right now. And Sean and Zach. Nothing else mattered but saving all of their lives. Hopefully helitack would be able to fly in and retrieve the two hotshots, but Megan and her children had no one to save them. Except for him.

Jared's vehicle bounced hard along the furrowed road as he searched for any sign of his green truck. Correction. Megan's truck. In his mind, he'd given it to her. Just as he'd given her his heart.

But where was she?

There! Her truck sat half-on and half-off the dirt road. Both doors stood wide-open. Megan and the kids were nowhere in sight.

He pulled over and got out, taking his Pulaski and fire shelter with him. Something had happened. He inspected the truck and discovered the problem. It'd become high ended when she'd tried to turn around. She'd probably been in a big hurry and couldn't get it unstuck.

"Megan!" he yelled, looking around for any sign of her.

They'd been here. He must have just missed them by minutes. The fire rushed nearer, moving so close that he could feel the heat of the flames blistering his exposed face. Billows of smoke flooded his lungs, and he coughed.

"Megan! Where are you?"

Where would they have gone? Where would she take the children? Not into the fire. And not back to the camp. She didn't have many options. He would have seen them somewhere along the road if she'd gone that way. Then where?

He paused. Within minutes, the entire place would be engulfed by flames. He had only moments to act. Whirling around, he ran toward the creek. He had to find them. Had to get them to safety.

"Megan!" he yelled over and over again. Desperate. Filled with fear. He couldn't lose them now. He'd given her his word that'd he'd keep her safe.

He yelled again and again. Hoping she could hear him above the roar of the fire.

This was his fault. His error. He'd promised she'd be safe, and he'd let her down.

* * *

Megan held her children's hands, looking for a safe place to cross the wide creek bed. The kids hugged close to her legs, terror filling their eyes. Drifts of white smoke shrouded Megan's view. Red flames winked at them. The fire was on the other side of the creek, too. They were surrounded. Trapped! So, where could she go? Maybe they should just get into the water and wait it out. That appeared to be their only option. But Blaine had told her stories of how the fire could superheat the water in a creek or stream until it was boiling hot. If they had a burnover, the creek wasn't necessarily the safest place to be. But what other choice did they have? She only hoped there was enough water in this wide creek to spare their lives.

"Megan! Megan!"

She turned, thinking her ears were betraying her. Thinking she'd lost her mind. Above the growling roar, she thought she'd heard her name, as if it came from a long tunnel. She paused, listening. Frantic. Desperate for escape. Her children's lives depended on her.

"Megan!"

There it was again! She was sure of it. Someone was calling to her.

"Here! I'm here," she screamed.

She peered through the smoke. A man's shape took form among the dry sagebrush. Tall and lean, moving fast as he ran toward her.

"Jared! Oh, Jared." She cried, falling into his arms. The children were crying, too. But he didn't pause for hello.

He pulled Megan's head close and spoke against her ear so she could hear him above the rumbling noise. "Take June's hand and don't let go. I'll take Caleb. Follow me."

He lifted Caleb on his hip. The boy held on like a python. Jared took hold of Megan's hand. Megan clasped June's wrist tightly. Then, she followed Jared as he stepped into the creek. The water rushed around their ankles, then their knees and thighs. They stumbled over the slippery rocks.

"But I can't swim. Mommy!" June cried.

"I've got you. I won't let anything happen to you," Megan said, pulling the girl onward.

Megan held tight to Jared's hand, hoping some of his strength might seep into her. To give her courage and hope. And that's when she knew. She needed to trust him. Completely. Since Blaine's death, she'd been living in constant fear. Cheating herself and the kids out of so much joy because she didn't want to be hurt again. But her plans to remain remote had backfired on her. She was miserable when Jared wasn't with them. So were the kids. They all craved being with him the way flowers craved rain. And now he was here. Her firefighter hero. As she uttered a quick prayer, she realized she trusted Jared completely. She trusted the Lord, too. Somehow, they'd get out of this alive. They just had to. She refused to consider any other option.

They waded into the deepest part of the water. It rose to Megan's waist and she held June close to keep the girl's head up. Jared did the same for Caleb. The man searched the embankment, though Megan had no idea what he was looking for. Finally, he pointed at a low overhang of plants where the roots had been washed free of dirt by the rushing tide. She didn't ask questions but trusted his judgment, going with him willingly.

He pulled them into the bank of the creek bed, pressing Megan and the children in against the damp earth. Then, he positioned himself with his back to the opening. As he shook out his fire shelter and wrapped it around them, his wide shoulders protected them. Whatever happened, he'd take the brunt of the fire. His heroism touched Megan's heart. He was prepared to die to save their lives.

Megan clutched folds of his shirt, pulling him closer. Trying to keep him safe, too. The children didn't move. Just remained silent, their eyes wide, their bodies quivering with fear.

Dead fish floated by. The water was quite warm. Not cold and clear as Megan remembered it from her fishing trips with Blaine. No, it was hot and uncomfortable.

"Mommy?" Caleb spoke in a frightened voice.

Megan was scared, too. More than at any time in her life. But she refused to give in to it. Even as the sounds of the fire intensified until it seemed a freight train was crashing down around them, she refused to let her fear destroy her.

"It's okay, sweetheart. We're going to be okay," she soothed her children. Hoping and praying it was true.

"Are we gonna die?" Caleb asked.

"Absolutely not," Jared said with conviction.

"Oh, Jared." Little June wrapped her arms around his neck and held on tight.

Megan leaned her head on the man's shoulder and closed her gritty eyes. A prayer stayed in her heart, begging God to save them. She wanted to cry but couldn't allow it. No weakness. Not now. Not when she had to be strong for her children. She had to fight. To trust. She had to!

"Hold on, Megan. We're gonna be okay," Jared said over and over again. And she believed him.

A shudder swept her body. She could barely hear him, the noise outside their tight cocoon sounded deafening. She knew it was the fire, burning through the trees and brush just above them. A burnover.

Jared's words gave Megan hope. The courage to ride out the storm and survive.

They didn't speak again. They seemed frozen in time. Locked in a bubble of angst and uncertainty. Unable to move. Unable to think.

They stayed that way for what Megan guessed was an hour before the firestorm passed and the loud sounds faded to a crackle.

"Look!" Caleb said. "A bug's crawling on me."

Looking down, she saw a small centipede was creeping along the sleeve of her son's shirt. She gave a croaking laugh, thinking how even the smallest of God's creatures must be frightened right now. They all wanted to live.

She brushed the centipede away and hugged her son tight.

Jared turned, moving slow and stiff as he peered out at the blackened ruins of the forest. "I think it's gone past."

"Can we get out of the water now?" June asked.

Jared nodded. "I think so, sweetheart. But stay close."

He edged his way out from beneath the overhang. The skeletal remains of blackened trees came into view. Drifting smoke had settled over the forest like a fat, dark cloud. Jared blinked his eyes and looked around. They all climbed out of the creek, their faces, arms and hands black with mud and soot.

Megan lifted Caleb onto her hip, her arms trembling with fatigue and shock. Jared picked up June. Together, they clawed their way up the embankment.

Voices filtered through the air. The whoosh of a water hose. The clamor of numerous men and vehicles working.

The smoke cleared, and Megan saw a pumper truck spraying the blackened remnants of trees, bushes and earth with a deluge of water.

The firefighters were here. And Megan

had never been so happy to see them in all her life.

She carried Caleb toward the thin road. The burned remnants of their trucks sat right where they'd left them. Megan shuddered when she considered what might have happened to her family if they'd stayed with their vehicle.

There were fire trucks parked nearby, while men scraped back smoldering bushes down to mineral soil. They shoveled dirt over the smoking remains of the fire.

"Jared!" A man waved at them.

"Come on." Jared took Megan's hand.

Megan struggled to walk, her legs weak and wobbly. She fell in the dirt, but strong hands were there to help her up. One man took Caleb, another one took June. Leland Churchill, the incident commander, greeted them, a relieved smile on his plump face.

"Boy! Am I ever glad to see you guys. We thought we'd lost you, too," he said.

"Too?" Jared said.

Leland's eyes filled with anguish, and he brushed a shaking hand through his short hair. He was a tall, strong man, but his eyes filled with tears. "We've got a couple of hotshots unaccounted for."

Megan froze, her heart up in her throat.

That horrible day when she'd lost Blaine came rushing back with the impact of a cyclone. She staggered, barely catching herself to keep from falling to the ground. Jared reached for her, wrapping an arm behind her back for support.

"Is it Sean Nash and Zach Carpenter?" he asked.

Leland nodded. "How did you know?"

"Dale Carter told me they were trapped. That a buttonhook fire had swept around where they were working. That's how I got the warning that I needed to come after Megan and the kids."

"Oh." Megan pressed her hand against her lips as she burst into tears. Sean and Zach were in danger. They might already be dead. It was too much. The horror replayed over again in her mind.

Jared held her close in his arms, his face pale with grief. In her mind, Megan could hear Sean's low voice and Zach's teasing laughter. Tessa must be beside herself with worry right now. The hotshots couldn't be dead. They just couldn't.

"I'm so glad you're safe," Leland said.

"Not half as glad as we are," Jared said.

Leland clapped Jared on the back. "As soon as the EMTs have a look at you, we'll drive you down into town. I'd like you all to go to the hospital to get checked out."

"Yes," Jared said. "Megan and the kids have breathed in a lot of smoke. I'm worried about their lungs."

"You will go with them. You've breathed in plenty of smoke, too," Leland said.

"I'm fine, sir."

Leland's jaw hardened. "I insist. I don't want to lose anyone under my command."

With that settled, two medics offered them first aid, then loaded them all into a truck. The ride into town was subdued. They shared two oxygen masks, but Megan was more concerned about her kids. And Jared. The man who had saved their lives.

The rest of the night rushed by in a blur. As Megan watched over her children, she couldn't help thinking about Sean and Zach, too. She carried a desperate prayer in her heart. That God would look after the two hotshots. That somehow, they'd get out alive and safe. And that He'd comfort Tessa as she awaited news of her fiancé and brother.

The doctors and nurses at the hospital offered the best of care. Administering bronchodilators for Caleb. Giving each of them oxygen and fluids. Washing the soot off their bodies. Making sure they were stable.

The next morning, once Megan knew they would be okay, she finally slept, sharing the same room as her children. She wouldn't leave their sides to save her life. And when she awoke, her weary mind wondered where they'd taken Jared. They'd faced death together and been handed a blessing of second chances.

Later, the kids were eating lunch when Megan left them for a time. Connie had brought her a change of clothes, so she cleaned up, dressed and then walked down the narrow hallway looking for Jared. She had to see him for herself. To know he was really okay.

She found him in a room down the hall, sitting in a chair as he tied his shoes.

"Hi." She smiled, slipping her hands into the pockets of her blue jeans.

He looked up, his face freshly shaved, his dark blond hair damp and combed into place. He wore a clean Forest Service uniform, and she thought maybe Connie had brought him a change of clothes, too. Except for the dark circles shadowing his eyes, he looked great. Never better. And yet, there was a forlorn look of misery in his bloodshot eyes that she didn't understand. She only knew that she felt a rush of gratitude so strong that she wanted to cry.

A sad smile curved his handsome mouth, but it didn't quite reach his eyes. He looked hesitant and uncertain. "Hello."

She stepped closer and rested her hip on a corner of the hospital bed. "Are you getting ready to go back out on the fire?"

He nodded and looked away. "They…they lost Zach Carpenter. Sean made it out okay, but Zach's gone…"

Jared covered his face with his hands. He didn't make a sound, but she knew he was crying. His shoulders trembled as the grief shook his body. Tears flooded her eyes, as well.

"Oh, Jared. Oh, no. I'm so very sorry."

She touched his arm, wanting to hold him tight. Wanting to run away at the same time. To flee and never hear such horrible news again.

"Poor Tessa. I should go to her. She'll be brokenhearted," Megan said as tears ran down her cheeks.

"Her mom should be here soon," Jared said. "They've pulled her and the rest of the Minoa Hotshots off the fire. Sean's being treated somewhere here in the hospital for some second-degree burns and smoke inhalation, but it looks like he'll be okay. They say he blames himself."

"Oh, no. Did he do something wrong to cause Zach's death?" Megan asked.

"Leland says no. Apparently Sean radioed the hotshot crew, giving them enough notice to evacuate. No one knows why he and Zach couldn't get out in time. But they'll send in an investigation team to determine what went wrong."

Yes, Megan remembered the same procedure after Blaine had died. The investigation team had found that he'd been working so hard that he hadn't noticed the winds changing and the fire creeping up on him. By the time he'd realized his error, he'd been surrounded. Human error, they'd called it. A simple mistake that had cost him his life.

Poor Zach. Poor Tessa and Sean. The three were inseparable. Sean and Tessa were planning to get married in the fall. So in love. So happy. And now this. Megan couldn't find words to say. Couldn't think this through. And yet, in her heart of hearts, she knew it would turn out okay. Because God was with them, no matter what. This wasn't all there was. Life went on eternally. Megan believed that with all her heart.

Jared looked at her, his eyes filled with anguish. "I'm so sorry for everything that happened."

"I know, but it wasn't your fault," she said.

"Yes, it was. I promised if you took the catering job that you'd be okay, and you weren't. You and the kids could have died…"

She interrupted him. "But we didn't. We're fine."

"But you wouldn't have been in that predicament if I hadn't pushed you to take this job."

"It was my choice, Jared. And I don't regret it, either. This job has blessed our lives. Financially, I'm able to breathe again. And it's allowed the kids and me to be near you."

A blank expression crossed his face. Then he nodded. "I don't want to lose you, Megan. I don't want to let you go. Not ever. I'll get a different job, if I have to. Nothing is more important to me. But you and I have to be together."

"We do?"

He nodded. "Yes, sweetheart. Because I love you. More than anything in this world."

"You do?"

"Oh, yes. And I love Caleb and June, too. I feel like they're my own children. When I thought I might lose all of you in that fire, I was beside myself with grief. I couldn't stand it, Megan. I had to save you. And if changing jobs will convince you that we should be together, then that's what I'll do."

A rush of happiness filled her heart. "That's good. Because we adore you, too. But I don't think it'll be necessary for you to get another job."

He stood and took hold of her arm, caressing her skin with his fingertips. "It won't?"

"No. It's enough that you offered. But when we were surrounded by that fire, something occurred to me."

He leaned near, until his nose brushed hers. "And what's that?"

"We need men and women like you, who are brave enough to put out the fires. Without you, there are a lot of people who would be in a whole lot of trouble. Because of your work, you save their lives and property. Just like you saved me and the kids yesterday."

He tilted his head to one side. "What are you saying, sweetheart?"

"I love you, too, Jared. I realize that now. I can't help it. I think I loved you the first time you stepped into my restaurant. I just didn't want to admit it. And I've been fighting it ever since. But now, I realize that life is too short to live in regret. That loving you makes me feel strong and fulfilled. It makes me a better mother. A better person. Like I can conquer any problem that comes my way. But only if you're by my side."

He gave a low laugh, as though he couldn't quite believe what she said. "I feel the same way. But do you really mean that, Meg?"

"Oh, yes." She didn't even hesitate. And she realized loving Jared meant more to her than being safe and lonely.

She loved him. With all her heart. And loving him chased away her fears. She wasn't afraid anymore. Even after what they'd gone through yesterday. Where there'd once been pain and anguish, now all she felt was calm, smooth peace in her heart.

"I thought the burnover would have pushed you even further away from me," he said.

"No, it's brought me closer. When I realized I could have lost you, it brought me to my senses. It made me realize I'd lose much, much more if I walked away from you. And I want to stay. To be a permanent part of your life."

Yes, the fire had galvanized her love for Jared. Because she realized, if she wasn't with him, life wasn't worth living anyway. Jared's love was worth any risk.

"Are you really sure? I mean, I know you still love Blaine," he said.

"Of course I do. He was my husband and the father of my children. I'll always have a place in my heart for him. But you're there, too. And I've learned that love isn't limited. It just grows and encompasses everyone I care about. My love for you is so powerful, Jared. I can't imagine living without you now. Oh, yes, I've never been more certain about anything in my life."

He laughed. "Then marry me. Be my wife and let's be a real family. You, me and the kids."

Megan hesitated. "Are you sure you're up to that? We're kind of a ready-made family. Our lives aren't always easy to manage."

"It's okay, sweetheart. Together, we can do anything. You're already mine. We were meant for each other."

"Yes, you're right. Life is too fleeting, and I don't want to lose anymore. Please don't quit your job. I want you to be happy, too. We've got a difficult road ahead of us now with losing Zach. Tessa and Sean are going to need our support. But managing fires makes you happy."

"But you make me happy, too. More than

I can say. You're the most important thing to me now. You and the kids."

She wrapped her arms around his waist and hugged him close. "I think we can have both. Just promise me you'll be careful out there. Promise me you'll come home safe every time. And after that, we'll exercise our faith in God."

He lowered his head, his gaze locked with hers. "Yes, I like that. I promise, sweetheart. I promise you that and all my love. Forever more."

He kissed her. And no more words were needed. Not for a very long time. Not until they told the happy news of their engagement to the kids. Because love truly was worth any risk.

* * * * *

Dear Reader,

I have a dear friend who is an ironworker and has walked the iron of numerous skyscrapers. My own father and other good friends have fought wildfires for a living. And I have a beloved son who is a Sergeant in the US Marine Corps. Brave souls, every one. They are my heroes. But I've often wondered how I might react if I were to lose one of them to their dangerous profession. Would I have hope and courage in the face of such adversity or fear? This is a question each of us must answer for ourselves.

In this book, Megan Rocklin's husband was a hotshot wildfire fighter who was killed in the line of duty. Suffering from a broken heart, Megan has vowed never to love another wildfire fighter, or any man who works in a dangerous profession. But I wonder if this is a realistic goal. Are any of us ever safe, no matter what we do for a living? Do we really know the day or hour when we might lose someone we love? For me, living by faith is the answer. Trusting in God and handing my fears over to Him brings me a great deal of peace.

I hope you enjoy reading this story, and I invite you to visit my website at LeighBale. com to learn more about my books.

May you find peace in the Lord's words!
Leigh Bale

LARGER-PRINT BOOKS!

GET 2 FREE LARGER-PRINT NOVELS PLUS 2 FREE MYSTERY GIFTS

Love Inspired®

Larger-print novels are now available...

LILP15

LARGER-PRINT BOOKS!

GET 2 FREE
LARGER-PRINT NOVELS
PLUS 2 FREE
MYSTERY GIFTS

Love Inspired.

SUSPENSE
RIVETING INSPIRATIONAL ROMANCE

Larger-print novels are now available...

REQUEST YOUR FREE BOOKS!

2 FREE INSPIRATIONAL NOVELS
PLUS 2 *FREE* MYSTERY GIFTS

Love Inspired® HISTORICAL

YES! Please send me 2 FREE Love Inspired® Historical novels and my 2 FREE mystery gifts (gifts are worth about $10). After receiving them, if I don't wish to receive any more books, I can return the shipping statement marked "cancel." If I don't cancel, I will receive 4 brand-new novels every month and be billed just $4.99 per book in the U.S. or $5.49 per book in Canada. That's a saving of at least 17% off the cover price. It's quite a bargain! Shipping and handling is just 50¢ per book in the U.S. and 75¢ per book in Canada.* I understand that accepting the 2 free books and gifts places me under no obligation to buy anything. I can always return a shipment and cancel at any time. Even if I never buy another book, the two free books and gifts are mine to keep forever.

102/302 IDN GH6Z

Name	(PLEASE PRINT)
Address	Apt. #
City	State/Prov.	Zip/Postal Code

Signature (if under 18, a parent or guardian must sign)

Mail to the **Reader Service:**
IN U.S.A.: P.O. Box 1867, Buffalo, NY 14240-1867
IN CANADA: P.O. Box 609, Fort Erie, Ontario L2A 5X3

Want to try two free books from another series?
Call 1-800-873-8635 or visit www.ReaderService.com.

* Terms and prices subject to change without notice. Prices do not include applicable taxes. Sales tax applicable in N.Y. Canadian residents will be charged applicable taxes. Offer not valid in Quebec. This offer is limited to one order per household. Not valid for current subscribers to Love Inspired Historical books. All orders subject to credit approval. Credit or debit balances in a customer's account(s) may be offset by any other outstanding balance owed by or to the customer. Please allow 4 to 6 weeks for delivery. Offer available while quantities last.

Your Privacy—The Reader Service is committed to protecting your privacy. Our Privacy Policy is available online at www.ReaderService.com or upon request from the Reader Service.

We make a portion of our mailing list available to reputable third parties that offer products we believe may interest you. If you prefer that we not exchange your name with third parties, or if you wish to clarify or modify your communication preferences, please visit us at www.ReaderService.com/consumerchoice or write to us at Reader Service Preference Service, P.O. Box 9062, Buffalo, NY 14240-9062. Include your complete name and address.

LIHI5